Unending
Havoc

Unending Havoc

Montana Mayhem
Book 1

Millie Copper

Copyright © 2021 CU Publishing
ISBN-13: 978-1-7353101-7-6

Written by Millie Copper

Edited by Ameryn Tucker

Proofread by WMH Cheryl

Cover design by Dauntless Cover Design

Also by Millie Copper

Havoc in Wyoming: Part 1, Caldwell's Homestead

Havoc in Wyoming: Part 2, Katie's Journey

Havoc in Wyoming: Part 3, Mollie's Quest

Havoc Begins: A Havoc in Wyoming Story

Havoc in Wyoming: Part 4, Shields and Ramparts

Havoc in Wyoming: Part 5, Fowler's Snare

Havoc Rises: A Havoc in Wyoming Story

Havoc in Wyoming: Part 6, Pestilence in the Darkness

Christmas on the Mountain: A Havoc in Wyoming Novella

Havoc Peaks: A Havoc in Wyoming Story

Havoc in Wyoming: Part 7, My Refuge and Fortress

Stretchy Beans: Nutritious, Economical Meals the Easy Way

Stock the Real Food Pantry: A Handbook for Making the Most of Your Pantry

Design a Dish: Save Your Food Dollars

Real Food Hits the Road: Budget Friendly Tips, Ideas, and Recipes for Enjoying Real Food Away from Home

Join My Reader's Club!

Receive a complimentary copy of *Wicked Havoc: A Montana Mayhem Prequel.* As part of my reader's club, you'll be the first to know about new releases and specials. I also share info on books I'm reading, preparedness tips, and more. Please sign up at:

MillieCopper.com/Wicked

Foreword

Montana Mayhem is a spin off from my previous series, *Havoc in Wyoming.* Though it is not necessary to read the previous series to enjoy *Montana Mayhem,* doing so will take you back to the beginning of the disaster and introduce you to the community and people of Bakerville, Wyoming. You'll also learn more about the women featured in Montana Mayhem and discover why each must find her way in this harsh, new world.

Who's Who

Tamra Nicholson: Twice-widowed mom of two daughters, thirteen-year-old Beth and seven-year-old Debbie. Her first marriage was built on love and trust—her second one, convenience and security needed at the end of the world. Now, what she thought was security, was nothing more than a lie.

Rochelle Bennet: Her son is missing. Her husband was murdered as she watched. She and her daughters were taken captive, then sold to the highest bidder. Now that Rochelle and her girls are free again, she's on a mission to find her son and bring him home.

The Hoffmann Family: Kimba and Rey Hoffmann, along with their three children—Nicole, Nate, and Naomi—fled Denver after the bridges exploded. They're invaluable members of the group and are committed to helping the other families reach their homes.

The Dosen Family: Away from home when the attacks started, Jennifer and her three sons are determined to return to their small ranch outside of Great Falls, Montana. Eighteen-year-old twins Atticus and Asher along with sixteen-year-old Axel have all trained with the militia alongside their mom. Will a few months of training be enough to see them safely home?

The Dawson Family: After her husband's atrocious acts made her family an outcast, Victoria Dawson and her two sons, Brett and Jameson, need a fresh start. They'll be joining the Dosen family in Great Falls—if they can make it there.

The Monroe Family: Skinny and malnourished, Leanne Monroe and her two children are last-minute additions to the group. Eight-year-old Sebastian has a ready smile for everyone, while his twelve-year-old sister Sadie keeps to herself.

Robyn Sorensen: After losing her only child last summer, Robyn was recently widowed when her husband was killed in a massacre. She now wants nothing more than to go home to the loving arms of her parents.

PJ Cameron: A close friend of Rochelle Bennet, PJ is committed to helping her find her teenage son. As a professional outfitter, he brings many skills to help on their journey, including a team of two half-draft horses and a wagon. But as they reach populated areas, will the wagon be a help or a hindrance?

Donnie McCullough: A bit of a rebel, Donnie is determined to help Leanne Monroe and her children make it to their aunt's home.

Tamra's Story

Chapter 1

June

"Is someone having a barbecue, Mommy?" six-year-old Debbie asks, looking up from the page she's coloring.

I stop my scrubbing and take a tentative sniff. With a shake of my head, I say, "It wouldn't surprise me. Lots of people are like us and only have an electric stove. Those stopped working when the lights went out, remember?"

"So they use their camp stove or barbecue grill," she says with a nod. "I remember."

"That's right, sweetie." I return to my cleaning. I'm on the last cabinet on this side of the kitchen, having taken everything off each shelf, giving them all a good wipe down before putting things back. I'm ready for a break as soon as this one's finished.

I started my cleaning frenzy a few hours ago, shortly after an argument with my husband left me with too much pent-up anger. While scrubbing, I've been replaying our conversation over and over in my head.

There're so many things I wish I would've said. But most of all, I wish he would've listened to me and did what I asked: put his wife and children first today instead of his job—a job he's no longer getting paid to do since the banks shut down when the power went out. Sure, they say they're keeping track of wages and will make things right, but will they? Dallas, my overly trusting husband, insists it'll be fine, they'll take care of us.

That man can be so infuriating! I understand he thinks he's needed at work—I not only understand but agree with him. But we need him here! With the world going crazy, and our little town starting to show signs of falling apart, he should be home with us.

"Tamra, honey," he said, reaching for my hand as we stood by his pickup truck.

I pulled my hand away.

He let out a sigh. "This isn't like you. Don't be like this."

"*Don't be like this?* After fifteen years of marriage, you should be the one not *being* like this. We need you here."

"Why? What is it you think I can do here?"

"You can keep us safe."

"You are safe. Look, I have to go. They're counting on me. With the hospital overflowing— " he shook his head " —they need me."

" *We* need you!"

He reached for me again.

This time, I let his fingers brush mine before pulling away.

With a hurt look, he said, "I'll be home when my shift is over."

"Doubtful," I spat. "You haven't been home on time since this whole mess started."

"Are you going to kiss me goodbye?"

I turned away from him, rushing back to the house and slamming the door. I leaned against the door, willing him to follow me. My chin dropped to my chest when I heard the truck start up.

"Nice, Mom," my older daughter, Beth, said. "I'm sure the neighbors heard you screaming at Dad." She turned and went into her bedroom. I haven't seen her since.

Letting out a long, slow breath, I begin replacing the dishes to the now sparkling shelves. I'm impressed how clean I was able to get everything with only a limited amount of water. When the power went out several days ago, the water stopped shortly after. There's still water in other parts of town, but not here. My husband has been good about bringing jugs home to us and making sure we have enough while he's at work.

Just a few days ago, things were normal. School was out for the summer. The girls and I were falling into a routine. As a stay-at-home mom since the birth of Beth, I try to make summers fun. Beth, turning thirteen in a few weeks, isn't making it easy this year. She wants nothing more than to stay in her room or play on her phone or chat on the computer instead of going to the park, the lake, or the host of other activities our summers usually involve.

I almost smile thinking about, until last week, that was the biggest issue in my life—my preteen daughter wanting to hole up in her room.

Now she still spends most of her time in there, but instead of being on her computer or phone, she's reading or just staring at the ceiling.

I wish the phones were working. I'd call Dallas and apologize. He was right when he said this isn't like me. Our marriage is a good one, and we rarely argue. And although I can get emotional—or as I like to think of it, passionate—I don't usually overreact. What's gotten into me?

I wipe my forehead with the back of my hand. It's hot today. And muggy. Wyoming's an arid area, and we usually have dry heat—dry cold too. The extra bit of moisture today makes it feel hotter than it probably is.

Maybe I'll go see Dallas during his lunch break and tell him how sorry I am for being such an emotional jerk, but also insist we need to talk about this and come up with a plan going forward. We've always been good at that—working together to do what's best. His logical side combined with my slightly more emotional side seem to complement each other.

"So, what's the deal with the toilet?" Beth yells from the hallway.

"Excuse me?" I call out. "If you have a question, please come and ask me properly instead of yelling."

With a huff and a puff, she steps just into my view. "Can I use the bathroom or not?"

I force a smile. "You may. Don't flush unless— "

"I know that part. But I thought Dad said it was getting backed up?"

I lift a shoulder. "We don't know. He was finally able to get it to flush last night. Just leave it for when he gets home."

With a flounce only possible by a girl her age, she disappears. Seconds later, the bathroom door shuts much harder than needed.

Beth was the first to find out about the original attacks. Dallas was home from work, having already put in a twelve-hour day as an orderly on the surgical unit of the hospital. We were watching a movie when Beth rushed into the living room.

"There's been a plane crash," she said. "Not just one but several. At different airports. They're calling it a terrorist attack."

"What?" I asked as Dallas grabbed the TV remote. "How do you know?"

"It's all over the internet. Everyone's talking about it."

We switched from the streaming service to a news channel, the three of us silently watching as the carnage was reported. I was grateful Debbie stayed asleep, especially when a reporter at one of the affected airports was doing a segment and a massive explosion interrupted the broadcast.

Soon, each of the airports that had plane crashes were in flames from secondary detonations. The worst part about the second explosions was they waited until first responders arrived—firefighters, EMTs, and police who were there to help. Thousands were killed.

It was terrible. But we weren't directly affected, with none of the airports being near us or anyone we knew being on a plane or near the explosions. Still, we mourned with the country.

Then, the next day, a second attack happened—or more accurately, a series of attacks—as bridges across the country were destroyed. Day after day, the attacks have continued, targeting oil refineries and train stations.

For reasons I'll never understand, scared people began fleeing the safety of their homes, which resulted in freeways and interstates, even small county roads, being jammed with travelers.

The TV showed roads in gridlock, and fuel trucks couldn't even get where they were needed to replenish empty stations. Then a nationwide cyberattack took out the lights, cell phones, home phones, computers, TVs, and more. Once that happened, things went bad fast, and now our small town of ten thousand is a mess too.

People are scared, and scared people can do awful things. Prospect, Wyoming, which is always busy during the summer with vacationers, is suddenly bulging at the seams as visitors to nearby Yellowstone National Park try to make their way home, only to end up stranded here because our gas stations are out of fuel.

I know Dallas is seeing some of the worst of it since his small hospital is overrun. Under normal circumstances, there are forty-five staffed beds with fifteen of those in the ICU. Now they're filled to more than four times their usual capacity. All elective surgery has been suspended, so Dallas is helping wherever he's needed, still in surgery sometimes since there's plenty of emergency cases.

Many of the injured are in the hospital after being attacked. Some were shot. Some were beaten. The hospital's generator keeps the surgical suites functioning, but Dallas says it won't last long. They'll soon run out of fuel.

Not only is the hospital overflowing with people needing care, but it's also set up as a refugee station. A soup kitchen operates out of the cafeteria, and people sleep any place they can find a spot in the building or on the lawn outside.

I get it. Dallas feels a need to be there, to fulfill what he thinks of as his obligation not only to his employer but to those he works with.

But as things deteriorate around us, I want him home. Especially after last night when we kept hearing gunshots. They were far enough away not to be a direct threat to us. But it was still scary. And we've been hearing about break-ins, not just at night but during the day too.

There's a knock at the door, quickly followed by, "Tamra! You in there?"

Debbie peers out the window. "It's Mr. Harv."

Swinging open the door, I don't even get out a hello before my retired neighbor yells, "It's the hospital! The hospital is on fire! I'm going to help. Candice will watch the girls if you want to come along."

He steps aside slightly to show his wife standing behind him.

"I'll watch the children, dear," she says, stepping inside.

"The hospital—how do you know?"

"Look!" Harv points to a huge plume of smoke. "Can't you smell it? Dirk was just here. They're rounding up as many people as possible to help. We need to go."

"I need a minute!" I cry, running to my room to slide into tennis shoes. My hands are shaking so badly, I can't get them tied. Leaving the laces loose, I race back to the living room. Beth and Debbie are sitting with Candice Murphy on the couch while her husband paces.

"Mom?" Beth asks with a quiver in her voice.

"Time's a wastin'." Harv strides toward the door.

I grab each of my girls, holding them tight while kissing them and admonishing them to mind Mrs. Murphy.

The fear in Beth's eyes is evident.

Debbie, who's still too young to really understand how devastating a fire like this can be, releases me. "Hurry home, Mommy."

I quickly slip out the door behind Harv.

When we reach the downtown area, traffic is heavy. We park several blocks away from the hospital.

"Grab those buckets." Harv points to an assortment of five-gallon and smaller containers. He grabs a shovel and bow rake before coming around the truck and taking a few of the buckets from me. "Can you handle the second shovel?" he asks.

With a shovel in one hand and four buckets held by the handles in the other, I awkwardly follow behind Harv. At his age, I'm surprised by how fast he's moving. While not running, he's definitely fast walking.

As we walk around a building, the hospital comes into view. I let out a cry when I see it. There're flames coming out of almost every part of the large building, and at least three lines of people—bucket brigades—are throwing water on the fire. My stomach falls as I take in the scene. The smoke smell, which was light at home, is almost overpowering here—heavy and acrid. How will a few buckets of water put out a fire that's already consumed more than half the city-block-sized building?

I frantically begin looking at the human chain, trying to find my husband.

"Let's take the buckets to the start of that line." Harv points to a group by a large portable cistern. After dropping off our buckets, Harv takes the shovels, going with a group that's trying to keep a nearby building from catching.

I look at the flaming building, the heat from it sweltering even at this distance. I need to find Dallas. I start off in that direction, then someone hollers about needing more people. With a shake of my head, I find a spot in the bucket brigade.

There's little talk while we work in the hot, ashy space. My eyes continuously dart around, watching the flame-engulfed hospital, trying to catch a glimpse of my husband. A makeshift triage area has been set up in a nearby park. Whenever I can, I look over there, trying to search out Dallas. That's probably where he is, helping move people around so they can get the care they need.

After many minutes, my shoulders ache from grabbing the bucket from the person behind me and passing it to the person in front of me. More than once I slosh the water, filling my shoe.

"Careful," the woman behind me hisses.

When I turn to get the next bucket from her, she's looking behind her, asking what the holdup is.

"Everyone, get back!" a voice near the front of the line calls out. "The building's coming down!"

The human chain breaks up, with people moving to the back of the line where I am.

"Oh, no," the lady behind me cries, wrapping her pudgy arms around her ample chest, rocking back and forth. "God help us." She crumples to the ground.

I sink to the ground next to her, tears filling my smoke-filled eyes as I watch the building begin to lean. A loud groan fills the air, then it's completely silent for many moments before the hospital falls.

"Do you know how it started?" I ask, my voice hoarse from the smoke, exertion, and disbelief.

"There was shooting and then— " She lifts her hands. "My son went in to help get people out. I don't . . . I haven't seen him."

"I'm sure he's fine. I'm going to look for my husband. He works here."

I offer the woman a hand to help her off the ground.

Once we're both standing, she says, "If your husband works there, he's probably at the triage area, right?"

"I think so, yes. That'd make sense."

"I hope you find him. I'm going up toward the front to see if I can find my son. God be with you."

"Uh, okay. I hope you find him." I jog to the makeshift hospital area.

A nurse I know catches my eye. She gives a slight shake of her head and a look I can't quite decipher.

I stiffen my back, walking toward her. "Is Dallas here?" I ask in a rush, my eyes darting around the area.

"I'll be right back." She gives a half smile to the person she's working on and then motions me to the edge of the space.

"What is it?" I blurt out.

Stepping close to me, in barely a whisper, she says, "I'm sorry, Tamra. He . . . did you hear about the shooting before the fire?"

I stop scanning the area and meet her eyes. "Yes. And?"

"Dallas—he was hit."

"Where is he? Are they operating—out here?"

"No, honey, he . . . Dallas is a hero. Even wounded and limping, he did what he could to help us get people to the stairs. But he was too injured. We wanted to send him down on a gurney, but he insisted we get the floor cleared first. I'm sorry. I don't think he made it out."

"You left him in there? To burn to death?" My voice is a high squeak.

"I'm so sorry." She touches my arm as someone calls her name. "I have to go. We'll have grief counselors here as soon as we can. I'm so, so sorry. Dallas was a wonderful man."

She leaves me there, staring at her. Another one of Dallas's coworkers looks up from the person she's tending to. She sees me and quickly breaks eye contact.

I run to her and scream, "Is it true? Did you leave my husband to die?"

"Tamra, it's not like that."

"Tamra!" a gravelly voice calls my name.

I whirl around. My heart skips a beat. They were wrong! It's Dallas! He's covered in soot and limping as he makes his way toward me. I begin to run. But after a few steps, I stop.

"Jackson," I say numbly. It's not my husband but his younger brother. From afar, especially with his face and clothes ashy, they look too much alike.

"Did you hear?" he asks, his voice thick and low.

"It's not true. They wouldn't just leave him to burn."

"The gunshot . . . they said he bled out before the fire."

He opens his arms to hold me, to comfort me. We grieve the loss of my husband, his brother, together.

Chapter 2

The following March

"Is this sliced thin enough?" I ask, lifting my knife and using it as a pointer.

Rochelle scrunches up her face. "Close. Maybe a little thinner on the next pieces. It'll dry faster that way."

I bob my head before slicing into the next piece. We work in silence for several minutes until the snap of a log in the woodstove causes me to jump. I drop the knife on the wooden table, and it slides onto the floor with a clatter.

"Oh! I'm—I don't know why I'm so jumpy."

"This world we live in, it's easy to react to every little sound."

"Are you worried?" I ask. "About what we'll find out there?"

She looks up at me, tears puddling in her eyes. With a shake of her head, she sets her knife on the table. "We probably have enough strips to fill up the bottom three racks. How about I put them on and then we'll take a break, have a good stretch and a cup of tea before going back to work."

"Good idea." I flex my fingers. "I feel like I've been hunched over this table for hours." I give a small, mostly fake, laugh.

"That's because, my dear Tamra, you have been! We both have. I may never be able to sit up straight again. We'll be thankful for our efforts soon. It'll keep us fed."

As Rochelle moves the thin pieces of venison to the newly constructed multiwire rack behind her roaring woodstove, I wrap the back haunch I was working on in a piece of cotton sheeting, then do the same with Rochelle's roast.

"I'm going to peek in on the girls after I put this away."

"Good idea," Rochelle says. "Tell them we're putting tea water on and to come over in fifteen minutes or so."

I give a nod before stepping out the front door of Rochelle's half of our duplex cabin. The bright sunshine reflecting off the snow is almost blinding. I take a moment to let my eyes adjust to the sudden change. "Wouldn't do to stumble and fall off the porch because you can't see," I mutter to myself.

After tucking the packages of meat into the cooler on the front porch, I stand and stretch, then shiver. I should've grabbed my coat. The calendar may show March 1st, but it's hard to believe spring could be anytime soon—not with several feet of snow on the ground and temperatures still well below freezing.

I shake my head. Two weeks until we leave. Maybe we'll get a warming streak before then. Otherwise, we could be making a mistake. I let out a snort. If only the weather was our main worry.

Closing my eyes, I take in a deep breath. Even in the cold, the smell of the woods is strong, rich. The woodstoves burning in the two dozen or so cabins add to the pungent aroma. There's something wonderful, almost healing, about living on the mountain. Or there could be, if I didn't have to deal with the other people living around here, if it was just Rochelle, me, and the children.

Like me, Rochelle is a widow. Also like me, she's a bit of an outcast.

But where I can't seem to focus on anything except the terrible things people say behind my back, Rochelle lets it all slide off her. She smiles and offers a kind hello, drawing out her critics, holding her head high. Maybe my oldest daughter is right. Maybe I'm just being a big baby about all of this and need to grow a backbone—or find the one I used to have.

Sometimes, I wonder how I've become this weak, insecure woman. There was a time when I would've walked up to one of those old biddies and gave them a piece of my mind, telling them exactly what they could do with their opinion of me. Not now. Now I'm so insecure I barely recognize myself. I need a change. A big change.

I turn toward the second door on the large porch—my half of the duplex cabin where the girls are hanging out while Rochelle and I work. The older girls spent yesterday helping us cut and dry the front quarters of the deer, while the two younger girls played games. Today, Rochelle and I decided they could have a break. Our decision was partly selfish to give ourselves some quiet time.

"Knock, knock," I say as the door opens with a creak.

"Hi, Mom." Debbie looks up from her game, lifting her hand in the semblance of a wave.

"Hi, Tamra!" Rochelle's youngest daughter, who's around the same age as Debbie, copies the greeting.

Rochelle's older daughter lifts her head from the daybed where she and my daughter Beth are looking over old issues of teen magazines. She smiles at me, while my own teen barely acknowledges I've entered the room.

"Everything going okay, Beth?" I ask my surly child—or as she prefers to be known at the tender age of thirteen and a half, young adult. Seems she thinks fourteen is the new twenty. And with the way things are, it's understandable—to a point. I still want her to be my little girl, to protect her and let her enjoy her youth. But Beth, like all the children and teens living in today's world, don't have the luxury of a carefree childhood.

"Fine, Mom." Without looking up, she turns the page.

"Did you go through those clothes and remove anything that doesn't fit?"

"Already done."

"Beth?"

"Yeah?"

"Look at me, please."

After a sigh that Rochelle probably heard next door, she says, "Yes, Mother." She purposely bugs out her eyes, exaggerating looking at me. "I went through my clothes and Debbie's. A few things fit them." She haphazardly motions to Rochelle's girls. "The rest can go to the supply house." Beth turns back to her well-worn magazine. "Don't worry, Mother. We know we can only take what we need to survive. We were at the meeting."

"Thank you, Beth." I force my voice to sound patient. *Kind.* Her life—all of our lives—has changed so much in the past nine months. And now we're making another change. "I appreciate you doing that. Did you start the list of things you'll need for the journey?"

Beth gives a slight lift of her shoulders. "Sort of. It's on the table."

"Will we need to take our summer clothes?" Debbie asks. "Last time we were at Grandma and Grandpa's when it was hot, they let me run in the sprinkler. But I don't have a swimsuit anymore."

She raises a valid point. Anything that fit last summer, she's long ago outgrown. "I'll see if I can trade for a few things at the supply house. Because we're taking the team and wagon, we'll be able to pack in a few extra things. But we can't go crazy."

"It's good we don't have to just carry our stuff on our backs." Debbie's eyes are wide. "That's what Naomi has to do. She can only bring clothes that fit in her backpack."

"Yes, having the wagon until we reach your grandparents' house is wonderful. You'll even be able to ride some. Naomi too."

She frowns. "I'd rather ski like you and Beth."

"You can ski in my place," Beth says. "I'd rather— "

"Yes, Beth." I muster every bit of patience I can find within me. "I know what you'd rather do. But once we get to your grandparents' home, to Joliet, you'll be glad we did it."

"I doubt that, Mother."

"We'll discuss this later." *A fib.* I have zero intention of doing so. We've already talked this to death. My decision is made. In two weeks' time we'll be leaving this mountain and heading for my childhood home in Joliet, Montana, whether my daughter likes it or not.

"And, Beth, please don't call me *Mother.* Mom, Mama, or Ma— even hey you would sound much nicer than mother said in that tone."

She lifts her hand and rolls her eyes. "Whatever you want."

I square my shoulders and give the girls a smile, one that Beth misses as she goes back to flipping pages. "Head over to the other cabin in about fifteen minutes. We're putting on tea and will have snacks."

"Are we eating something good, Mommy?" Debbie asks, stressing calling me mommy in a sweet voice while widening her eyes.

I move to the kitchenette. "We got home-canned applesauce in our rations this week. How does that sound with mint tea?"

"Did you get cheese?" Rochelle's youngest daughter asks. "We got cheese this week."

"We did," I say. "But we had that last night before bed."

"We haven't had ours yet. Maybe my mom will share with you if you share applesauce with us?"

"Sounds like a plan." I give her a smile. "So we'll see you in fifteen minutes. Right, Beth?"

"Yeah, no problem."

Back in Rochelle's cabin, I don't even say hello before I start lamenting on my teenage daughter. "I don't know what I'm going to do with that girl. She's so . . . so negative all the time. It's like she goes out of her way to be difficult." I drop my chin to my chest and whisper, "I know she has her reasons."

Rochelle offers a sympathetic smile. "None of this has been easy for any of us, with everything that's happened nationally, locally . . . personally."

"Your girls seem to be handling it well. And with what they've been through—what you've been through—I'd think they'd be acting out too."

"Oh, believe me," Rochelle says, lifting her hands, "we have our days! When I start noticing the signs, I try and listen to the Lord, leaning on His Word to determine how I should respond. It's not always easy." She gives me a smile.

I take a deep breath and force myself not to roll my eyes. Surely, I can act more mature with my good friend when she starts spouting off about her newfound religion than my teenage daughter does with me. I paste a smile on my face. "I'm glad you've found something that works for you. This new faith of yours seems to give you, um, comfort."

Rochelle returns my fake smile with a real one of her own. "God has become the most important part of my life. Through Him, I'm learning how to be a better mom."

"Are they angry at you? Your girls? For leaving them, I mean."

Her smile falters. "It's not going to be easy. I know that. We've discussed the dangers. And they've seen enough in the months since the attacks started and the EMP hit to be concerned. But they both understand I have to go. I must find their brother and bring him home so we can be a family again."

I give a nod. "And you feel God is leading you in this. You've said you prayed about it."

"I do. Even though it's a risk and I know things might not work out as I hope—*as I pray*—I also know I might not make it back and my girls will be orphans. Even so, I can't not go."

"Don't you think it might be smart for us to wait and leave after the snow's gone?"

"When will it be gone?" she asks with a mischievous twinkle in her eye. "This is not only the apocalypse but the snowpocalypse! I've never seen anything like this. I mean, sure, we're living on a mountain at high elevation—a former ski resort—so there should be snow, right? But even the lower elevations, back in Bakerville . . . " She bites her top lip. "I hope things are going okay there today. Such a terrible, terrible thing."

We move to the couch near the woodstove. My part of the duplex is a studio with a queen-size bed, a daybed with a trundle underneath, a loveseat, and a chair plus the small kitchenette and a bathroom. Rochelle's side is a one bedroom, with twin beds in the bedroom and a queen bed in the living room, plus a sofa bed, kitchenette, and bathroom. The woodstove in this larger cabin warms both of our spaces, with the addition of several vents at the top of the shared wall.

"Are you expecting PJ to be back today?" I ask.

"That's what he said. If he's back early enough, he wants to have another planning meeting, ideally before supper so we can attend the church service after we eat."

"He'd better hurry then. It's already after three." I point to the windup alarm clock sitting on her side table.

"How about you? How are you feeling about leaving?"

"Scared. But excited. What was that show about those oil drillers going into space? One of them said he's 95 percent excited and 5 percent scared. Or maybe it's the other way around and 5 percent excited and 95 percent scared. That's how I feel."

"I love that movie," Rochelle gushes. "My heart was pounding during most of it. Watching movies and reading books about the end of the world was much more exciting than living it."

"Yeah, I definitely liked it when those scenarios were purely fiction. Living it's not that great." I give her a weak smile.

"Exactly. And that heart-pounding action in movies and books, I don't want that! Now, the less excitement the better. Instead of nonstop action, I want boring. I want to not have to worry about making it through each day, about being attacked."

"But we're putting ourselves out there by leaving the safety of the mountain. We know how dangerous it is. I mean, look at what happened to those that stayed behind in Bakerville instead of moving up here with us. They're dead."

"You could stay here, Tamra. No one's forcing you to go. Wait until later, after the president has his reconstruction efforts in place and travel is safer."

I let out a sigh. "I know. I've thought about it. But I don't know if I can handle one more day of judgmental looks and talk about me and my girls behind our backs. I'm not like you."

At her raised eyebrows, I quickly add, "I mean, there's still a few who blame you for what happened, right? A few who think Fred was really innocent and you made it all up? But you don't worry about them."

"Sure, I guess. But those few—you're right, I don't put much stock in their opinions. You shouldn't either. How were you supposed to know your husband was a killer?"

Chapter 3

I stare at Rochelle. The brutal way she says it, that my husband was a killer, stings. She's right, I didn't know. I had no idea. The discovery was not only shocking but heartbreaking—and another life-changing blow in a terrible series of events. Last June, my life was normal. *Happy.* Dallas, Beth, Debbie, and I had a great life full of joy, laughter, and friends.

Then Dallas died in the fire. His brother, Jackson, offered to take the girls and me to his house in the small enclave about a half hour north of our town of Prospect. But I didn't want to leave my home. Plus, I needed to make funeral arrangements.

Jackson understood. He stayed overnight, grieving with us. And what a night it was. Not only were we mourning, but the entire town had gone nuts with shooting and screaming so loud—and close—it made sleep impossible. Not that I could sleep after the death of my husband.

Did it all stem from the fire at the hospital and the overwhelming grief our small town was experiencing?

The next morning, Jackson asked again. After the night of bedlam, the only choice was for me to take the girls and flee to the isolated community of Bakerville, Wyoming.

"We'll give it a few days," Jackson said. "Let the worst of it pass and then I'll bring you home."

"Okay," I said. "We'll need to make arrangements. Do you think . . . will there be a body for us to bury?"

With his face filled with grief, he shook his head. "I don't know. But we'll do something, a memorial, when things calm down."

When we started packing, it was just a couple of bags for the girls and me, then Jackson would suggest something else. Eventually, my car and Jackson's pickup were full. With the grocery stores and every other store in town closed, we brought every scrap of food in the house, Dallas's guns and ammo, extra clothes, and shoes—Jackson even said we might as well grab our winter coats since nights can sometimes be chilly, even in June.

With the nationwide fuel shortage, I was extremely grateful my husband always insisted we keep our tanks at least half full. Jackson was down to a quarter tank, so he siphoned from our quad and also took the small gas cans from the shed. Harv Murphy promised to keep an eye on our home for us while his wife gave the girls and I goodbye hugs.

"Don't worry," Candice said. "I'm sure everything will calm down within a few days. We'll help you plan Dallas's funeral."

"Our son Dirk said there's talk of a community memorial next week sometime," Harv said. "Give it a few days for the havoc to subside."

Jackson's small home was very private and quiet. Nestled near the national forest on a forty-acre parcel, it was a good place to grieve. When the phones started working a few days later, I tried to reach my parents but couldn't get through.

I did reach Candice, who said she thought the worst of it was over. "With the phones working, even though not reliably, people are a little less crazy. There's talk things will soon return to normal. Not a moment too soon either. I was starting to worry about Harv. He'll run out of his heart medicine in another week and then . . . anyway, the memorial will be on Thursday."

It was time to go home to Prospect. Attend the memorial for my husband and the hundred or so others lost in the fire, then try to piece together some sort of new life. I'd need to find a job.

Then things changed in an instant.

My smartphone pierced the quiet of a Sunday morning with an urgent signal. The United States was under a missile attack, and we were told to find immediate shelter. The girls and I were alone in Jackson's home, cowering in a small windowless bathroom, hiding in the tub, waiting for the missiles to strike.

They never did. Not in Bakerville, anyway. We found out later there were nuclear ground detonations on both coasts, destroying many of the port cities. For the rest of us, a nuke—or maybe several— was set off at high altitude, resulting in an electromagnetic pulse.

An EMP.

It was the coup de grâce. The death blow.

Jackson returned several hours later—having to walk when his truck stopped running, never to start again—to find us still huddled in the bathroom. We had no idea what was happening. It wasn't until the next day when his friend Fred stopped by, telling us we'd been nuked and that the accompanying pulse meant almost everything with a computer chip was gone for good.

He'd seemed almost giddy about it and kept calling it the "Great Reset." Fred, a Prospector County deputy sheriff, said he had a lot of training about life after a nuclear blast. "Survival of the fittest, that's what this will be," he said. "You watch. In a couple of years, we'll emerge from this stronger. Now's the time for people like us to stand up and lead."

I was too numb to even think about what he was saying at the time. But now, I'm haunted by his words and demeanor, about his excitement over the reset—Jackson's too.

There was a gleam in Jackson's eyes as they talked about how it was their time. After Fred left, Jackson took notice of my distress, holding me while I cried. At that moment, I longed for my mom, to have her hold and comfort me. I wished I would've asked Jackson to take me to my childhood home instead of staying with him.

Only two short months later, I became his wife.

"That sounded a little harsh, didn't it?" Rochelle whispers, bringing me back to the present. "I'm sorry, I should've thought first instead of just blurting that out."

I raise a hand. "It's certainly no worse than what others say."

"Except I'm your friend. We've shared so much." She shakes her head. "Besides, I don't know why you worry so much about what they think. When I met you, you were tough as nails—a little too tough maybe." She gives me a smile and waggles her eyebrows. "I was in awe with the way you carried yourself, your presence."

I tilt my head and answer with a slight nod. I don't tell her that, when I met her, I made up a nickname for her in my head: Reclusive Rochelle.

That meeting was supposed to be a party, a barbecue to get to know each other and celebrate Labor Day—not that there was much to celebrate in our new world. Dallas had died only a couple of months before. But by then, Jackson and I were a couple and planned to get married.

I was so embarrassed about marrying my brother-in-law, I even asked my children to lie about it, to pretend Jackson wasn't their uncle and that he was just my boyfriend. And they definitely couldn't tell anyone Dallas had died such a short time before.

Rochelle was living with Fred Lassiter, Jackson's good friend. And to my knowledge, she was happy with him and also wanted to get married. The get-together was not only to celebrate the holiday but to begin discussing a double wedding for Rochelle and Fred plus Jackson and me.

Rochelle was so quiet, she barely responded when I spoke to her. And when she did talk, it was in a whisper, so I only heard every other word. I'm not going to lie, it was a miserable time. When we left their house, I told Jackson I didn't care if I ever saw *Reclusive Rochelle* again.

He repeated the name, raising his eyebrows and using a disgusted tone of voice.

I made an oops face. I hadn't intended to tell him about the less-than-kind nickname. It just sort of slipped out. Creating nicknames is something I've been doing for years— probably since high school. Not all of them were mean spirited like Rochelle's was.

Dapper Dallas was what I called my husband because he was so handsome, so perfect in my eyes. I made a mistake of sharing a less-than-flattering moniker with Dallas for one of his coworkers. He wasn't impressed, telling me it was childish and judgmental, not to mention cruel. How would I feel if *blah, blah, blah.* Sure, I knew it wasn't kind, but did it really hurt anyone?

After that, I didn't tell Dallas about the little names I'd come up with in my head. And when Jackson asked, I brushed it off and tried to explain how she seemed so quiet and how talking to her was a challenge.

And I certainly never told Jackson I'd had a nickname for him as well: Don Juanson. He'd had so many girlfriends over the years, without ever settling down, the little play on the name seemed to fit. Turns out, although the name of a legendary scoundrel was somewhat fitting, Jackson the Ripper would've been spot on.

I nod at Rochelle. "Yeah, well, I was putting on a good show for sure. Even though I knew it was smart to marry Jackson, I was still so raw from the death of Dallas. You know what that's like, especially since you were a new widow yourself."

"Yes, but neither of us knew the other one was still so fresh in our grief. Fred— " She makes a face. "He said you and Jackson were a perfect couple who had been in love for years."

"I know. And Jackson said you had just lost your husband but the two of you were estranged, that he was Fred's cousin and . . . anyway, we were both covering up lies. You married Fred so you could stay alive and care for your girls. I married Jackson for security, a way for my children to be cared for."

"Understandable," Rochelle says. "We do what we need to do to take care of our children. Going after Christopher— " She lets out a sigh. "I know it's slightly nuts. I'm leaving my daughters here, to be cared for by others, while I go in search of my son. But how can I not? I need him with me. Or . . . " She forcibly swallows. When she speaks again, there's a quiver in her voice. "I need to know. If he didn't survive, I just need to know."

A pounding at the door causes both of us to jump.

Chapter 4

With a self-conscious laugh, Rochelle says, "See, you're not the only one who jumps at everything."

"Do you think . . . should you get your gun?" I ask.

She lifts the tail of her shirt slightly to show the handgun on her hip. "Maybe tomorrow we'll have time to work with you on your pistol, get you comfortable carrying it." She goes to the cabin door and calls out, "Who is it?"

"PJ."

Her face breaks into a smile as she throws the door open. "You're back!"

With his hat in his hand and his broad forehead glistening in the bright sun, he says, "I'm back."

Rochelle immediately picks up on the sadness in his voice. "Was it rough?"

"Terrible."

"Do you want to come in?"

"I need a shower. The, uh, the pyre—the smell lingered. Permeated. I need to get it off me. I just wanted to tell you we're back and that I'd like to have a planning meeting tonight. Does after supper work?"

"You want to skip the church service?" Rochelle asks.

"If you don't mind. There're more people who want to join us."

"Who?" Rochelle asks, leaning against the door frame.

"Robyn Sorensen. Her husband was among those killed in the massacre."

The massacre. It's odd how we now describe events. *The attacks. The EMP. The insurrection. The serial killings.* The massacre is the latest in a string of heartbreaking disasters.

Two weeks ago, a group from our community left our mountain to goose hunt in the basin and along the river, what many refer to as Bakerville proper. What they found when they reached the town was dead body after dead body. Five young children, who were in an unexpected place when the killings began and managed to hide, were the only survivors.

I don't know Robyn Sorensen but know there were a handful of women who moved up the mountain with their children while the husbands stayed behind to care for their property. She must be one of those.

"How many children does she have?" I ask from my place on the sofa.

PJ squints and leans his head inside the dark cabin. "Hello, Tamra. I didn't see you there."

"We're working on the meat." Rochelle motions to the strips behind the woodstove. "Well, we're taking a break at the moment, just finished slicing and salting this batch. We did some by the firepit this morning. We both have the day off, so we're taking advantage of it."

"A full day off, huh? That's a rarity." He gives Rochelle a crinkly smile.

It's no secret how they feel about each other. Well, no secret to anyone but Rochelle. With all she's been through, she's not ready for anything resembling a relationship. But that doesn't change the fact that she has feelings for him. She doesn't admit it, but it's obvious.

And he's head over heels for her. Why else would he volunteer to escort her on this journey to find her son? He knows as well as anyone, better than some maybe, about the dangers of this world.

"We only have about half of the two rumps remaining," Rochelle says. "Those make the nice strips. We cut all the leg meat off and dried it at the firepit. It'll be a little chewier. But if we heat it in water, it might make something resembling a soup."

"Yeah, that'll work. I think we'd better harvest another deer with as big as our group's getting. Anyway, we need to interview them and vote. Only two weeks until we leave. Not a lot of time for them to get ready."

"You didn't answer how many children Robyn has," I remind him.

"No children—not living, anyway. She and her husband lost their only child last summer to some kind of allergic reaction or something. It's just her."

"Where's she going?" Rochelle asks.

"To a little town outside of Billings. It shouldn't be too far out of our way."

"Where will we meet?" I ask. "If they're having church, we can't meet in the ski lodge."

"Thought we'd meet at the other lodge. One of the folks living there has been helping with the cleanup and moving things from the river up to the mountain. I asked him on the way home. He said it'd be no problem."

I give a nod. I've heard of meetings in the dude ranch lodge. Some of the support groups meet there, and the former town council met there. But that was before.

"Hi, Mr. PJ," Debbie calls out. "Are you having tea with us?"

"Not today, Miss Deborah. You gals enjoy your tea party." He looks to Rochelle. "So after dinner tonight? We'll meet Robyn and the others, then vote."

"Who are the others?" she asks.

"We'll meet them tonight."

~~~~

Even though Rochelle's daughters will be staying with a friend instead of joining us on our journey, they still attend the planning meetings. Rochelle says it's because the girls are helping her get supplies together. I know that's true, they are, but I think it's also because she wants to spend every possible minute with them.

I can't even imagine what she must be feeling. The choice between leaving her daughters behind, knowing there's a chance they could become orphaned, or not going after her son and never knowing what's become of him, that's not a choice any mother wishes to make.

PJ's already in the meeting room when we arrive. Standing next to him is a tall, mousy looking woman with long black hair hanging limply around her elbows. She was probably overweight before everyone went on a forced diet, and she's still what my mom would call big boned.

I'm tallish, at five-seven, but she's a couple of inches taller than me, close to PJ's height of somewhere around six feet. Where she's stout, my body is more athletic—not a body shape I've ever been fond of. There were many times I wished for a womanlier figure. And these last several months of forced rations haven't done anything to help that. At least I'm not overly scrawny.

Rochelle, who's not only shorter but shapelier than I am, walks over to her and offers her hand. Next to the petite Rochelle, the woman is positively ginormous. "You must be Robyn. I'm Rochelle."
~~~~

Robyn manages a smile and mumbles, "Yes, we've passed in the food line."

"I'm surprised we haven't been on any work crews together."

"I'm on modified duty crews, have been since last summer." Robyn's voice is a sad whisper.

Rochelle gives her an understanding nod. We have a psychiatric nurse—essentially a shrink—who often changes duty assignments if she believes someone's mental health is suffering. There're even a few people she's put on suicide watch, which isn't surprising since we're all depressed to some degree. She's even tried to talk to me, to get into my head. I'm not at all interested. I can handle my issues on my own.

"You're going to Billings?" Rochelle asks Robyn.

"Lockwood. It's outside the city. My parents retired there. Um, that is, if you'll have me."

"We'll wait until everyone arrives." PJ motions to the door. "Then we'll talk about it. You'll need to tell us why you want to go and what you bring to the group—the things we talked about." He nods as he speaks. "Then you'll step out and we'll vote."

"I understand." Robyn drops her shoulders, seeming to fold in on herself. She suddenly seems much smaller.

Several catchy nicknames run through my head. Since I no longer think of Rochelle as Reclusive Rochelle, she could easily become Reclusive Robyn. It's evident—I stop myself with a shake of the head. Somehow it feels wrong to give this obviously grieving woman any sort of nickname. I mean, who wouldn't be grieving after losing their child and husband?

I reach out my hand. "I'm Tamra. I'm going to Joliet."

"I know." She limply takes my offered hand, dropping her gaze.

Okay, fine. Maybe she *will* get a nickname.

"Hello!" Kimba Hoffmann, her husband Rey, and their three children stride confidently into the room. I'm convinced that's the only way the family knows how to move—confident, self-assured, and perfect. Always perfect.

It's not just how they move but how they almost look like a family of supermodels. Even the youngest girl, who's around Debbie's age, carries herself with an air of confidence. She gives Debbie an enthusiastic wave before joining her and Rochelle's daughter at the sofa in the corner. The two older Hoffmann children, a boy around

Beth's age and an older teenage girl, smile their hellos before finding their own seats.

"The Dosens should be here shortly," Kimba says. "We ran in to Jennifer at dinner. She said she has an errand to run first."

"Yup," PJ says. "Do you know Robyn Sorensen?"

As PJ makes the introductions, Robyn does her best to put on a friendly face.

"We've met before." Kimba returns the smile. "Last summer, we did some cross training on the militia teams."

"I . . . uh, yes. I'm not on the militia now."

"I know. Please accept my condolences for the loss of your husband."

Robyn drops her gaze and responds with a single bend of her neck. "We had the memorial yesterday. I wish . . . I would've liked to bury him next to my son, but with the frozen ground . . . "

Kimba takes both of Robyn's hands in hers. "I heard from others it was a beautiful ceremony. And there's talk of setting up a plaque or something for remembrance?"

"Yes, someone mentioned that. But not until after things return to normal."

There're several beats of silence before Kimba pulls Robyn into a hug. "I'm praying for you, praying you'll feel God's love and He'll give you peace."

Robyn begins to cry as she thanks Kimba over and over.

Feeling terribly awkward and out of place, I move to the corner where the youngest girls are chatting. After many minutes, the door opens again, allowing more people to spill in.

It's a group of three brothers with weird names, twins around eighteen years old and another a few years younger, sons of Jennifer Dosen. I don't even try to remember the boys' names, or which is which. They all look enough alike, tall and blond just like their mom. They look so much alike, I've decided it doesn't really matter which is which. Plus, it seems over the last few months, as our world has gone nuts, remembering names is just too much for me. Somedays, I can barely remember my own! Oftentimes, I even call my girls by the wrong name.

Debbie gets a kick out of me mistakenly calling her Beth—not so much with Beth being called Debbie. That usually garners me an eye roll and a reminder that I've messed up again. I don't know what it is.

My mind doesn't seem to be as sharp as it once was. It seems getting through each day takes all my energy. Adding in anything else . . . I can't do it.

But as far as these three brothers go, I'm not the only one who can't keep them straight. Many in the community have taken to calling them *The A Team* or *The A Boys* since their unusual names all begin with A.

"Where's your mom?" Kimba asks one of the brothers.

"Getting her snowshoes off. And visiting. You know how she is."

His mom's a talker, always going out of her way to chat someone up. Not me, of course. But I've seen her do it with others. I barely knew her before she joined this traveling group a few weeks back.

Rochelle and PJ had been making plans since the first of the year, but they didn't tell me about it until early February. Rochelle knew I wanted to get home to my parents and very kindly offered to help.

Her timing was perfect. I'd just finished a kitchen shift—one of the work crews I'm on—where someone muttered a less-than-kind comment about me followed by a dirty look. I was at the end of my rope and completely desperate to leave this miserable mountain and these intolerant people. Had we been able to, I'd have packed up right then and there.

It was a few weeks later when the Hoffmann and Dosen families joined our trek. The Dosens have a small ranch outside of Great Falls, Montana. It's northwest of the Billings area, so when we reach Joliet, the Dosens and Hoffmanns will head west while PJ and Rochelle go east to her son's summer camp.

The Hoffmann family met the Dosens last summer, making a pact to help get them home. At the time, the Hoffmanns were going to Bozeman, Montana, where they have friends. Now they're committed to getting Jennifer and her boys all the way home. It's over two hundred miles from Joliet to Great Falls—weeks of traveling on foot. I'm not sure I'd be as willing if it were me. No way would I want to be traipsing all over the state with my children if I didn't have to.

Kimba and Rey don't even seem bothered by the thought of going out into the world. We've all heard stories of the dangers. And we know what happened to the people in Bakerville.

The president has made a few announcements over the radio. He assures us things will soon be back to normal, that he's working on getting the lawlessness under control and the lights back on. *Reconstruction efforts* is what he's called them.

The Hoffmanns say, once they get Jennifer home and check on their friends in Bozeman, they plan to help with the rebuilding efforts. They feel it's their calling or something. Of course, the life they led before everything collapsed might be why they're so enthusiastic about being involved with the government.

"Here we are!" Jennifer Dosen sticks her head in the door.

A chorus of greetings welcome her.

Another head pops into view. I narrow my eyes. I recognize that matted, filthy hair. Icky Vicky Dawson.

Chapter 5

"Goodbye, Lily! Bye, Sissy!" Debbie calls out as she waves. "We're leaving pretty soon, and I get to ski down the mountain!"

"Maybe," I say quietly as her friends run toward her, expressing awe over her proclamation.

Debbie ignores me and keeps talking to the friends she's leaving behind about what an adventure she'll have. As excited as Debbie is, Beth is more on the side of melancholy. At least she's stopped being quite so churlish and smart-mouthed with me.

This came about after taking snowboarding lessons with Kimba and Rey Hoffmann's oldest daughter. I guess their daughter is super excited about the opportunity to be part of the rebuilding of America. She said she knew it was a risk to travel away from the safety of the mountain, our home for the past six months, but she has a chance to be a part of history.

Beth perked up slightly after that, especially when the seventeen-year-old expressed interest in Beth and said how great of friends they'll become while traveling together. After that, there was a new glow to Beth and, likely, a case of hero worship.

I don't have the heart to tell Beth we'll be holing up in Joliet and not inserting ourselves into any rebuilding efforts, not unless there're things that happen right where we're living and are safe. But I'll take the truce we seem to have.

This morning, as we were checking our cabin to make sure we had everything, Beth even apologized to me, telling me she knew she was being rotten and she wanted to stop blaming me—not only for leaving the safety of the mountain but for everything that's happened since her dad died.

Our talk definitely lifted a little weight off my shoulders. It also made me miss Dallas even more. I wish he was here, with us as we embark on this possibly dangerous endeavor.

At the moment, Beth is quietly talking with the few friends she's made since we became official members of the community last fall. Even though we'd been living with Jackson since the end of June, few people knew of us until mid-September.

At first, I was grieving too much to care about seeing anyone. Then Jackson started hearing things about how the women and children were forced to work in the fields under the blazing sun, treated essentially like slaves. He had stories about some of them passing out from exhaustion and dehydration. I didn't want that for my girls or myself. And since no one really knew we were living with him, we just kept it quiet.

Rochelle's fiancé, Fred, was doing the same thing, keeping quiet about her and her girls. Although people knew she was living in Bakerville, he said they were in no condition to help with community work after the things they'd been through. It wasn't a complete fabrication. Rochelle and her daughters *had* been through an ordeal, but it wasn't any better living with Fred Lassiter.

"It's getting to be about that time." Jennifer Dosen sidles up to me. "Did you say all your goodbyes?"

"I'm not close friends with anyone except Rochelle and her daughters."

She gives me a smile. "Rochelle is one of the bravest women I know."

I tilt my head at her. "She's been through so much."

"Oh, yes. Definitely. But this—going after her son and leaving her daughters behind—what a brave and difficult thing to do."

My eyes move over to Rochelle, where she's making a last-minute adjustment at the wagon. Or maybe it's a sleigh since it has skids added to it to make traveling through the snow easier. Whichever. She'll be riding on the seat, trading off with PJ, driving the team or riding shotgun. Although she grew up around horses and has been riding for most of her life, she'd only driven a team a few times in parades and other events, so she's had lessons to make sure she knows what she's doing. PJ says she's a natural. Rochelle insists it's the amazing half-draft horses that make it easy.

"You feeling confident on your skis?" Jennifer asks.

"Ha. No. Even with the lessons and practice, I'm still clumsy. You?"

"Better. You know, a year ago, I was so overweight I never would've thought about doing something like this. Backcountry skiing isn't something I would've considered fun."

"I don't think it's going to be that much fun. Weeks of skiing and, um . . ."

"Skinning."

"That's a terrible sounding term."

"I know!" She laughs. "I keep telling my boys that, but they insist it's correct. We'll be following each other's skin trails."

"Skin trail. That sounds even worse."

When we first started talking about leaving this mountain hideout, I thought they'd give us snowshoes. Nope. They offered us backcountry skis.

At first, I didn't understand how they thought skis would help us. I mean, skiing off the mountain if it was all downhill, sure. Maybe. But what about the other areas? Even on the mountain there are buttes. And once we reach the basin, we'll be on flat farmland. With several feet of snow on the ground, during a record-breaking winter— if anyone's still keeping records—we'd have a terrible time walking.

Then they explained the backcountry skis get these strips of fabric attached to them, called skins, which help with walking. The ski and skin combination works something like snowshoes to keep us above the surface, and the skins grab on to the snow to give traction.

Skins, called by the name because they were once made out of animal skins but are now synthetic, are sticky on one side to help adhere to the ski. The other side goes on the snow and glides along. Or at least it's supposed to. Although I've been practicing for several days, I've yet to master the skinning process and spend more time stumbling over the skis than gliding.

"The hardest position is the beginning of the line, just like with snowshoes, when you're breaking the trail," Jennifer says. "But at least we should have a bit of fun on the downhill slopes."

"I don't know about that. Even though I've ran down the bunny hill a few times, I'm not sure how steady I am skiing. I'd hate to fall and break my leg."

"True. Kimba and Rey have backcountry skied before. They'll make sure we don't do anything too steep."

"And your boys, do they ski? Or snowboard? Most of them are on snowboards, right?"

"Splitboards, yes. They pull apart and work just like our skis during the skinning time, but then they can put the two pieces together to make a snowboard. Beth is on one of those too?"

"She is. And to quote her, 'It's pretty cool.'"

"No doubt! Sounds just like my boys. Ah, there's Victoria. Looks like she's ready now."

My eyes follow Jennifer's gaze. We agreed to accept Icky Vicky Dawson and her two teenage sons into our group. I'll admit, I was shocked when she appeared at our meeting, especially because Jennifer and her boys were the ones inviting them along. That was a complete surprise, considering Victoria Dawson's husband staged an insurrection that was responsible for the death of Jennifer's sister and several others.

"Do you want to walk with me, make sure Victoria and her boys have everything they need?"

"I'll stay here so Debbie can visit with her friends as long as possible. We should be leaving soon."

"I'd think so. Looks like everyone's here, including our latest additions."

Not only did we agree to have Robyn Sorensen and Victoria Dawson's family join us, but a few days ago another woman with two children asked to come along.

I wish I would've voted no on that one.

Having just arrived in our community last month with another group, I'd heard a few rumors about the woman, about how she was hateful to everyone. But she was apparently on her best behavior during the interview. While she didn't smile or chitchat, she was at least cordial. I thought maybe the gossip was just exaggerated, similar to what I've experienced.

But after we voted her in, her true colors came shining through. And not in a good way.

"Is it about time, Mom?" Beth asks.

"Yeah, I think so. Debbie, tell your friends goodbye, then let's go over by the wagon."

"Who's that?" Debbie asks, pointing to a man walking a saddled buckskin.

I let out a sigh. "He showed up when we were packing the wagon last night while you were visiting your friends, right around the time it started snowing. We decided to let him join us."

"Why didn't I get to vote?" she asks with a pout.

"I told you about him, remember?" Beth says. "He's coming along because he's friends with that Leanne lady and her two kids."

"Her name is Mrs. Monroe, and I'm pretty sure her daughter is around the same age as you," I say quietly to Beth.

"Yeah, well, she looks a lot younger than me, and she never talks. As far as I'm concerned, she's a kid. Anyway, as I was telling Debbie— " Beth shoots me a look " —he wants to make sure they get to where they're going. PJ and Rey thought it might be a good idea to have another shooter."

"They didn't say shooter." I shake my head.

"But that's what they meant. They wanted someone comfortable with a gun, not someone who's new to carrying one." She points at the gun on my hip, then moves her finger upward to the rifle hanging from my shoulder by its sling.

I feel the blush start up my neck. "Say your goodbyes, Debbie. Beth, let's move over to the wagon."

~~~~~

Glide . . . don't lift. Glide . . . don't lift. I blow out a breath, coating my sunglasses with fine mist. Just the momentary distraction causes me to clomp instead of glide. Shaking my head, I return to my mantra.

"You doing okay?" Donnie McCullough, the last-minute addition to our group, asks from atop his horse.

"Fine," I answer.

"You sure? Looks like you're floundering a bit. You want to call for a break?"

"I'm fine."

I feel his eyes boring into me, looking down on me, but I keep staring straight ahead.

Glide . . . don't lift. Breathe normally. Don't let him hear you gasping for air. "Keep in mind, all you have to do is sit. I'm using my own energy."

"Hey, I'm not denying I have it easier. I'll ride my horse any day." He makes a noise with his mouth, then he and his horse bound to the front of the skin trail.

We finally left the lodge just before nine this morning. I was surprised by the number of people who showed up as we were trying to hit the road. Almost everyone stopped to say goodbye. Not to me, really, though there were a few people who seemed to go out of their way to wish me and my girls well. At least Debbie and Beth felt truly loved.
~~~~~

"Won't be long now," Jennifer Dosen calls from behind me. "We're making great time and should have another decline in a few minutes. I'm pretty sure I can see it ahead."

Making great time? Our pace is anything but swift. At least the weather is clear and crisp. It started snowing last night, and I was worried it'd turn into another arctic blast. But this morning, we woke to sunshine—a bluebird day. It wasn't even very cold, at least not by Wyoming standards. It was probably midtwenties, without a lick of wind. A dry cold. Comfortable.

I clomp again, this time almost stumbling. Biting back a sigh, tears sting my eyes as frustration runs through me. Or maybe it's fear. The last thing I need is to fall and break my leg. And then what? No doctor. No help. I'd be done for.

Riding a horse or riding in the wagon-turned-sleigh, like Debbie and the younger children are, would be so much easier.

What I'd really prefer is a vehicle—one of the double cab pickup trucks!

We could load it up and get where we're going in no time. But running vehicles are scarce, and fuel is precious. And considering the community wouldn't even allow us to take snowshoes, there's no way we'd ever be allowed a truck. There was even a huge debate over taking the team and wagon. Several people were very vocal with their opinions, declaring we could walk out with the clothes on our backs and nothing more.

PJ made a strong argument for taking the wagon and horses: his family owns them. Or at least they *did*, before they arrived in the community of Bakerville and agreed to contribute all usable belongings to the good of the community.

Socialism—that's what Jackson kept calling it. The requirement to give up private property to community ownership can't be considered anything else.

"Woohoo!" someone calls out. "We're just about off this flat and ready for another downhill run!"

"All right!" someone else exclaims. "I'm ready to ride!"

"Hold up, everyone," one of the A Boys says as he unhooks the sled he's towing. "Let's take a break while we get the skins off and get ready for the descent."

I continue my glide to where the A Boys are already stopped. Jennifer effortlessly glides in behind me. Beth is already stopped, sipping on some water. The rest of the on-foot group is either chatting or drinking from their water bottles.

"Whoa!" a call goes out, bringing the wagon team to a stop.

I awkwardly clomp to a stop next to Beth and quickly pop off my skis. I fix a fake smile on my face. "Whew. Feels good to get those clumsy things off. How are you holding up?"

She peels off her heavy gloves and removes her knit cap, shaking out her light brown hair that's damp from the exertion. "It's fun." Her smile is genuine. "It isn't hard with the gentle uphill and the flats, but it's kind of weird to get used to walking with skis on. At least the skins give good traction. Axel says there's only one steep uphill on this entire road. We'll reach it before the end of the day, then tomorrow should be a piece of cake."

"Which one's Axel again?" I ask.

"The youngest of the A Team."

"Oh . . . " I give her a slow nod, then whisper, "You mean the cute one?"

She shoots me a look and then makes her eyes go wide.

I let out a low chuckle. "Did he say that? Piece of cake?"

"I wish he wouldn't have mentioned cake. It got us talking about food, stuff we probably won't ever have again. Now I can't stop thinking about it. Chocolate cake with a thick layer of fudge frosting."

I pat her hand. I'd love a piece of cake too—carrot with cream cheese frosting. I bite back a sigh. "Things may change, Beth. And about the uphill, keep in mind, it's followed by a long, steep decline. We'll probably keep the skins on for a good portion of it, walking down instead of skiing. It's safer that way."

She shrugs. "It might be dangerous on skis like you have, but I'm on a snowboard—much safer."

"I don't know about that. Besides, you've only been snowboarding for a couple of weeks. Just since we started planning this— "

"Exile?"

I tilt my head. "I was going to say trip."

"Sure, Mom." She gives me a slight eye roll. "Trip. We'll call it that if you want."

Although she's been considerably better in the days leading up to our departure, she still can't help but sass me when given the opportunity. I start to reprimand her when she raises her hands. "Just kidding, Mom. It was a joke."

"Hmm. Thanks for telling me it was a joke. You rest. Drink some water. I'm going to check in with your sister."

"You know she's going to want to ski down."

"I know," I answer with a slight sigh. Even though they ride in the wagon on the flats, Debbie and the Hoffmanns' youngest daughter have skied down the previous two slopes. I'd much prefer they stay in the wagon.

For that matter, I'd much prefer walking down the slopes instead of going through the rigamarole of repurposing our gear for skiing instead of skinning. It's such a pain to take off the skins, stow them in our packs, adjust the bindings, then do the reverse after finishing the run. Of course, we're at the bottom of the hill much faster than the wagon, so we do have time to get the skins back on and even rest before they catch up to us.

But there's an inherent risk to all of it. Any of us could stumble and fall. I'm just glad I don't have to drag one of the sleds down with me. Then I'd definitely worry about falling.

I awkwardly move toward the wagon. These boots aren't made for walking, not elegantly anyway. Even with them switched to hiking mode, which makes walking easier than regular downhill boots, they're still cumbersome. The rockered rubber soles do a fine job of gripping the snow, and they aren't heavy, but it's still different than wearing regular snow boots.

"Hey, Mom." Debbie waves vigorously from her spot under the blankets. Three other little heads also poke out, their faces red from the cold.

Leanne Monroe, the only adult in the well-packed wagon, sits separately from the kids with a permanent scowl marring what could be an attractive face. She makes sure to shoot me an extra dirty look just for good measure.

I'm tempted to stick my tongue out at her. But with the children watching, I give a slight narrowing of my eyes before turning my head and smiling at my daughter.

"Time for me to ski?" Debbie asks.

"Me too?" the Hoffmann girl asks.

"We'll probably have a break first?" I direct my question toward the front of the wagon.

"Yup," PJ answers. "The horses need a break. We might as well take an early lunch."

Although there were several very outspoken community members who didn't think we should be allowed to bring provisions with us, the majority were willing to give us what we needed.

Just a few days is all it should take. We'll be off the mountain and back in the community of Bakerville by tomorrow evening. From there, it's just over forty miles to my parents' home in Joliet. What would be a short drive by car will take us around a week of trekking through the snow.

A pang of worry courses through me. We're taking a chance, a chance my mom and dad will be able to welcome the girls and me with open arms. I shove the thought aside.

"C'mon out of the wagon," I say to Debbie. "Let's walk around a bit before lunch."

Chapter 6

The ground's mainly level now that we're off the mountain, but the snow has drifted in places, making skinning a challenge. We've been swapping off leaders to keep from tiring out any one person. I've only been at the front for a few minutes, and my legs are already burning.

It's day two of our journey to Joliet. Last night, crammed in a much too small two-person backpacker's tent, the girls immediately fell asleep. I wish I could say the same. Though physically exhausted, my mind wouldn't shut off.

I'm starting to think we've made a mistake, that Beth has been right all along: I impulsively decided to come on this journey based on my hurt feelings. It would've been smarter to stay on the mountain, to wait until we know it's safe to travel.

I guess I'm having some sort of traveler's remorse. It doesn't help that I couldn't get warm last night. That certainly made sleep difficult. While better than nothing, the tents aren't even close to being rated for this weather. It may be shelter, but it's far from cozy. At least they're light enough to carry in the backpacks and keep us out of the elements, but barely.

The gear we're using—my skis, Beth's splitboard, the modified skis Debbie has, the ski poles, tent, sleeping bags, pretty much everything—will be handed over to Leanne Monroe, the nasty lady riding in the wagon, and her children when we arrive at my parents' home. Even though Leanne insisted on coming with us, the medical team on the mountain tried to convince her neither she nor her children were physically up for this trip. The three of them are malnourished and underweight, and walking across a state wouldn't help that. The compromise was they'll ride in the wagon until they have to walk.

Giving up our tent and gear isn't a big deal. There's no reason for us to have these things since we won't continue past Joliet.

As long as my parents are able to take us in.

Without working phones, there's no way to know if they are well or even alive. And thinking of my parents takes me right back to where

I was last night when I couldn't sleep. What was I thinking bringing my girls on a journey like this?

There's so much violence in the world right now. No place seems safe. The quiet, sleepy town of Bakerville wasn't spared from the bloodshed. It's naïve of me to assume my parents' town of Joliet was protected.

"Ach!" I cry out as I cross my skis. Flailing my arms, I barely prevent myself from going down.

"Whoa, there." The boy skinning behind me grabs my arm. "You okay?"

"Fine, yeah. I'm fine."

"Do you want me to take the lead? You can step out and fall in at the back."

I agree and step aside, waiting for the line to go by until I'm at the end. I now have the worst spot: behind the sled Rey Hoffmann's pulling. I concentrate on gliding and not clomping.

Tonight, instead of tent camping, we're staying in a house in Bakerville. Last fall, around the time Jackson and I were married, most of the people in the small community relocated from the basin to the mountain. The small, contained ski lodge was determined easier to defend than the spread-out area of Bakerville.

Jackson and I discussed staying at his home. We thought Fred and Rochelle would also stay behind. In the end, our deciding factor was our lack of food and supplies. Plus, neither Fred's nor Jackson's homes were set up to survive a winter without power. Of course, we know now, after the massacre of those who stayed behind, we made the right choice.

The house we're staying in tonight is in a different area from the murders, a place belonging to a friend of PJ's dad. Although it likely won't be too comfortable, since it hasn't been occupied since last fall and we don't know exactly what we'll find, I'm sure it'll be better than sleeping on the ground in a tiny tent with two squirmy children—warmer too.

Maybe I'll feel better about this journey after a good night's sleep. *Humph.* Not that it matters. It's not like I can just turn around and go back to my little cabin.

"PJ's calling for a quick break," Donnie McCullough says as he rides by on his horse. I still contend he has it easy, but I must admit, having him on this trip is helpful. He's able to keep everyone well organized and pass messages along.

Leanne, however, doesn't think much of him being on this journey. Last night, she started off being short with him and rapidly progressed to downright angry. Seems she's angry at him for even being here. Although she admits they're friends, I guess their friendship doesn't extend to traveling across the state of Montana. She certainly gave him an earful, causing him to sulk the rest of the night.

This morning, he was still acting a little hurt but seemed to, once again, go out of his way to talk to Leanne and be around her at breakfast. It's very weird.

"It best be a quick break." One of the A Boys motions to the sky. "We're going to get snowed on."

"Really?" I ask, looking around. "It's beautiful. Not quite as nice as yesterday, but still . . . "

"Snow's coming." He points behind me.

I turn to look back up the mountain, toward the ski lodge we left yesterday. A haze covers the area and limits my view. Letting out a sigh, I ask, "How long do you think?"

"An hour, two maybe."

Leanne rolls her eyes and mutters, "What do you know, kid?"

"Atticus just seems to know things," his mom, Jennifer, offers with a lightness to her voice. "Even when he was young, he'd know if a storm was brewing or . . . well, other things. My husband used to say he had a direct line to God."

"Humph." Leanne snorts. "Obviously, he didn't know about the end of the world coming, or else you wouldn't be stranded away from home."

"Well . . . " Jennifer lifts a shoulder.

"Can I get you some more water, Mama?" Leanne's son asks. He, Debbie, and the young Hoffmann girl are all around the same age.

With a small smile and slight nod, she hands him her insulated bottle. "Thank you." She touches her son's skinny arm.

"You must've been super thirsty." He gives his mom a wide smile. "You drank yours quick."

Our stop is brief, just enough time for a snack and water. When we're getting ready to go, Kimba Hoffmann says, "It doesn't look like anyone's been here since the last snow. I don't see any new tracks."

"Good deal," PJ says. "We haven't been down here since the memorial service. It's snowed a few times since then, so . . ."

"Right." Kimba gives a solemn nod. "That last storm should've dropped enough snow to cover up the evidence. We'll still want to be cautious."

"Always cautious, love." Kimba's husband, Rey, wraps an arm around her shoulder. "Donnie can take the lead. Kimba, you mind being the first of the walkers? Atticus and me, we'll pull up the rear just in front of the wagon. How do you feel about riding shotgun, PJ?"

"And let Rochelle handle the team?" PJ asks.

"Right. Have your rifle at the ready, just like in the old west."

Rey and Kimba Hoffmann are in charge of security for our group. On the mountain, they were part of the advanced group of our militia. Even though he's only eighteen, one of the A Boy twins was also on their team. Almost everyone else was in the regular militia, or was at one point. Not me, and not Icky Vicky Dawson, but the rest of the adults in our group and even the older children were.

The Hoffmanns are trained well beyond anyone else in our group of refugees—well beyond most in Bakerville even. From the rumors I've heard, they have quite the sordid past as spies or some kind of mercenaries. Maybe both.

One day last summer, when we were still living in Jackson's small house, he came home talking about how this couple with three kids showed up in town. One of the retired townspeople held them at gunpoint. He was so tickled by the event, he kept replaying it over and over for days, sharing all the new rumors that came out about the three of them being in a spy ring—maybe for the government, maybe for some black ops group.

Even now, I think of Kimba as *Kimba the Spy* and her British-born husband as *Secret Agent Rey.* Jackson's gossip about them and the lady who held the gun on them was nothing compared to how the kitchen crew carried on. Man, could some of those people blab. It'd be funny if I wasn't also a source of their scuttlebutt.

Back on the skis, I'm following Beth. We're moving faster than before the break, spurred on by the impending weather and the excitement of reaching the end of today's trek. While the others have weeks or months of travel ahead of them, I'm grateful the girls and I will only need to walk—*or skin*—another week or so.

After only a few minutes, Donnie, who'd ridden ahead, returns at a trot and calls for a halt.

"What's going on?" Kimba asks, as Donnie walks the horse toward us.

"The ground's scuffed ahead. Looks like one person. The tracks are just shy of the corner." He gestures to a gentle bend in the road. "Looks like they turned around and walked back. Maybe a sentry?"

Kimba lets out a sigh. "It was too much to hope we'd have this easy."

Chapter 7

"Is it just tracks in the snow?" Rey Hoffmann asks. "Or something dodgy?"

"I didn't see anyone," Donnie says. "But they're fairly fresh."

"Everyone move behind the wagon." Rey motions. "Let's put something between us and them."

Instead of turning on my skis, which is always a clumsy endeavor, I unlatch the bindings and leave them in place, telling Beth to do the same.

PJ turns the wagon at a slight angle to give us more space to get behind.

"The children?" I ask.

"In the wagon. Nate, you get in too," Rey directs his preteen son.

"But, Dad— "

"In the wagon. Rochelle, be ready to hightail it to the mouth of the canyon if things go bad."

PJ and Rochelle share a look. She gives a nod.

"We'll go check it out," Rey says.

Kimba shakes her head. "And I was hoping for an easy trip."

"Oh, darling, you should know better." Rey gives her a wink.

"Can we at least make it fun?" she asks. "We could take the skins off and pretend like we're wearing race skis."

"We'll be just like Bond, James Bond." Rey waggles his eyebrows at his wife. "You think you can shoot while on the skis?"

"I think you know the answer." She smirks at Rey before turning to the rest of the group. "Donnie, pop Asher on your horse and both of you head over to the grove of trees." She points to a line of trees near the bend in the road.

"Before you go," Jennifer Dosen says, "Atticus, please pray."

"Our dear heavenly Father," he starts with barely a pause, "please keep us safe from harm. Let whoever made those tracks be gone, or at least friendly. Please let there be no bloodshed today. In Jesus' Holy Name, amen."

I mumble an amen along with everyone else. Religion isn't my thing. Not even close. But if they think praying will help, then fine. I'll let them pray. I'll even join in.

"Okay," Rey says. "We don't know what we're going to encounter, so everyone needs to be ready." He spends a few minutes instructing people where he wants them.

My name isn't mentioned. I let out a quiet breath. I hate that, even though I have a rifle slung on my back and a pistol on my hip, Rey doesn't include me in the instructions. Jackson forbade me from joining the militia. And then, after everything came out about what he did, I was too embarrassed to ask to be a part of the team.

Last month, after the Bakerville massacre was discovered, there was a new urgency with training and security. I'd already started planning with Rochelle to leave the mountain, so why bother with the training?

Even though I wasn't a part of their precious militia, I'm not totally inept. Dallas made sure I knew how to shoot a rifle and a pistol, the same ones I'm carrying.

"Okay, folks," PJ says quietly after Rey and his group head out. "Let's get the children in the wagon and then get set."

"Mom?" Debbie calls to me with a quiver in her voice.

"We're going to be fine. Mind your sister and stay down."

"We're fine, Mom." Beth wraps an arm around her sister.

"If there's gunfire, will the horses bolt?" one of the older children asks.

"They shouldn't," PJ answers. "They've been around shooting all their lives. I was a hunting outfitter, and they were with me when out hunting. Even when they're ground tied, they're good at standing still. Let's everyone get in position. Use the ditches and the few boulders to your advantage. Tamra, you know what to do?"

"I'm good." I hide my smile. While the militia people may have ignored me, PJ was able to spend time with me as part of our preparations, so I'm confident with both my pistol and my rifle.

With ammunition being limited, we only had six live rounds for my 9-millimeter. Most of our time was spent dryfire practicing and running through different scenarios. One of the more stressful exercises was when he'd tap my shoulder and I had to draw my weapon and fire four times fast. We did it over and over, and it was what we used four of the six rounds for. The other two, I'd shot off first just to make sure I was on target.

As I make my way to where I'm stationed, I think of our motley group and assorted defensive weapons. Most of our crew is outfitted in a similar manner as I am: a sidearm on their hip and a hunting or predator rifle slung on their back—mine is Dallas's Steyr Scout chambered in 6.5 Creedmore—along with at least one knife tucked somewhere. My knife is in a sheath and tucked in the pocket of my snow pants, easy to get to but not too obvious.

A couple of the teenage boys carry shotguns with defensive loads. PJ has them stay by the wagon to defend the younger children. A few, like Kimba the Spy and her husband Secret Agent Rey, carry high-capacity tactical rifles.

As I settle in, I glance back at the wagon. Beth lifts her hand in acknowledgment. I blow her a kiss. She rolls her eyes.

I move onto my stomach, stationed behind a boulder on the side of the road. The forestock of the Scout rifle opens to become a bipod, making shooting prone easy and convenient. While PJ helped ensure I was proficient during our practice sessions, I don't want to shoot. I hope this is nothing more than a false alarm.

Kimba and Rey have gone around the bend and are out of my view. Everyone else is set up, waiting.

The wind picks up, making lying on the cold, snowy ground uncomfortable. My multiple layers and water-resistant outer shell may soon be of little help.

As the clouds overtake the sun, a drizzly snow starts. I'm starting to shiver when Donnie leaves the thicket of trees. He mounts up while the teen who was with him takes off on foot, stumbling through the deep snow, toward where I last saw Kimba and Rey. I turn to look at PJ, who motions me to wait.

As soon as he's within shouting distance, Donnie calls out, "We're fine. Let's go on to the house."

"Was it a false alarm?" I ask.

"C'mon over here, Donnie." PJ motions. "Let's everyone gather around."

At the wagon, Donnie says, "It's a couple of guys. Rey made contact and determined they're not a threat."

"Really?" I ask. "He's sure?"

"Seems so." Donnie bobs his head up and down. "It's just a couple of transients heading north. They stopped here for a few days during the cold snap, harvested a deer and are taking time to smoke it. They invited us to have stew with them."

"Humph," Leanne says from her spot in the wagon. "Sounds suspicious to me. No one gives anything in this world without expecting something in return."

"How far is it to the house?" Rochelle asks.

"A mile, maybe less." PJ turns back to Donnie. "Where're they staying?"

"The community center," Donnie answers. "Isn't that right next to your friend's place?"

"Yeah, across the road. Why there? Why not use one of the houses?"

"Don't know." Donnie gives an exaggerated shrug. "You can ask them over supper."

Chapter 8

With a fire roaring in the woodstove, the longtime unoccupied house moves from freezing to only slightly warmer, still cold enough to see our breaths.

While a few people are on watch, many of us huddle around the small stove, willing it to warm our bodies. Tonight, I'll have a watch shift. My first. Since I wasn't part of the militia, I was never on sentry duty like most of the others in our traveling group.

When we were on the mountain, the older boys—girls too—were all part of the militia, taking watch or sentry shifts regularly. Everyone age sixteen and up were full militia members, while those fourteen to sixteen were what they called runners or junior militia. Beth would've been a runner in just a few months.

Up till now, she'd spent her days in the makeshift school, but at the age of fourteen she'd be encouraged to start an apprenticeship and have official militia training consisting of more in-depth firearms practice and additional hand-to-hand combat training. While the apprenticeship would include basic education, I'd much prefer her to keep up with her book learning, especially considering last month our ham radio picked up a transmission from the president, assuring us things would soon return to normal.

Back to normal means high school and college, not shooting bad guys and fighting for her life. I just hope the months she hasn't been in regular school haven't set her back too much. Even though they did have some bookwork, too much of their day was spent learning things like animal care, starting fires, building shelters out of twigs, self-defense, weaponry, and other things that may be necessary at the moment—in this life we're forced to live—but won't be once the president turns the lights back on.

I glance over at two of the younger boys; they're fiddling with one of the projects they made in school: slingshots. Beth and Debbie made these too, all the students did. Constructed from forked branches they dried near the firepit and then notched and smoothed, many were a work of art. Adding the rubber from old tire tubes didn't do much for the looks, but the pouch—made from a goat skin they tanned and tooled as desired to hold the projectile—gave the students another opportunity for expression.

"They're heading this way," one of the boys calls from where he's keeping watch. Although I've yet to meet the guys holing up in the community center, Jennifer said they seem nice enough, maybe a little on the eccentric side. When I asked what she meant, she said, "You'll see soon enough."

A few minutes later, Kimba is ushering them inside. On first impression, I immediately agree with Jennifer. While one of them looks like your average end-of-the-world guy, the other certainly stands out. Like almost all the men in today's world, both are fully bearded, on the long and scraggly side—a common look.

The one takes it a step further with his hair fashioned in two Willie Nelson style braids ending at his elbows. He's wearing a red snowmobile suit that looks like it's from the '80s or even older. With his age being somewhere north of sixty, he may have even been the original owner of the hideous ensemble. As if the bright red clothing isn't enough, he's topped his head with a red stocking cap. Nothing like being fully visible in this white world.

Jennifer opens her hands to receive the soup pot Willie Nelson is carrying.

He nods his thanks. "Brought y'all a jug o' water. Wasn't sure how y'all were fixed for fluids, and figured ya might need time to get snow melt goin'. Got it in my haversack." He motions to a bag slung over his shoulder.

"That's very kind of you," Kimba says. "We started a couple of pots to boil, but it won't be drinkable for a while."

"Makin' water's a full-time job during the winter." He pulls a well-worn plastic soda bottle from his bag. "Melt the snow, boil water, let it cool. Takes time fo'sho. We did try an' break the ice on the creek, but the cold blast was a doozy. Ice so thick ya can walk on it."

I give a nod. I was often on the water crew at home. We broke the ice off a patch twice a day to pump out water. Even then, it'd often freeze almost solid between retrievals. "What about where the creek meets the river? Is it frozen there too?" I ask.

"Not sure. Din't feel like venturing to find out. And we're 'bout ready to hit the road again. Our meat's mostly taken care of. Made some jerky and cut and froze the rest. Not hard to do in this weather, but gettin' it thawed to cook may take some doin'."

"Do I hear Alabama in your voice?" Icky Vicky Dawson asks, with a slight southern sound to her own voice.

"That's right, ma'am. Born and raised. Though, I've been workin' in Texas the last few years."

"And you?" Victoria asks the other one, who has yet to speak.

"Colorado."

"Name's Scruff," the Willie Nelson one says. "He's John. We met up outside of Craig, Colorado. Heading the same ways, so figured we might as well travel together."

"Scruff's a funny name." Debbie laughs.

I make a shushing sound at her.

"Well, it is," she whispers.

"It is a funny name." Scruff kneels down on one knee so she can see his face without craning her neck. "My name's surely Marcus, but the onliest one to call me that was my ma. And then jes' when I was in a speck o' trouble. Folks gen'rally call me Scruff since that's what my older brothers called me. I'm the young'st of eight, and by the time my ma had me, her arms were so full of other babies she just carried me around by the scruff of my neck like a kitten."

"No way!" Debbie's eyes go wide.

"Well, that's the way I heard it enway." He gives her a wink before returning to his feet with a moan and several creaking bones.

"That's quite a story, Mr. Scruff," Kimba says with a laugh.

"Just Scruff, ma'am."

"All right." Kimba then goes around the room introducing each of us. From the glazed looks on Scruff's and John's faces, I suspect neither will be any better with names than I am. Maybe that's just how it is at the end of the world. Does it really matter what anyone's name is?

"Where are you going?" Debbie asks.

"Canada. Heard things might be normal there—or somewhat normal. Thought I'd give 'er a try. John here's just looking for a new start. Not sure where he'll end up. Ain't that right, John?"

John lifts a single shoulder.

"You're going to a whole other country?" Debbie asks, her voice full of disbelief. "Why are you doing that? The president was on the special radio. He's making things normal again. Did you hear him?"

Scruff shrugs. "Why not? Nuttin' keepin' me here. Always wanted to go to Canada. Be quite the adventure. And normal? *Ha.* We'll see."

"We're going on an adventure too," Debbie says.

"That's right, Debbie," Kimba says. "We already told Mr.—um, *Scruff* about our trip plans."

I feel my eyebrows shoot to the top of my head. *They told a stranger about our plans?* Kimba catches my reaction and gives me a serene smile.

"Yep. Yep, they did." Scruff strokes his beard. "Wondered if y'all might consider lettin' us tag along part-uh the way."

Rey clears his throat. "I'm not sure how that might work."

Once again, my eyebrows shoot up in surprise at Rey's voice. Usually laced with a mild and pleasing British accent, he sounds like a Midwesterner with little variance in intonation. This time, Kimba winks at me. *Okay . . .*

"Understand," Scruff answers with a slow nod. "All y'all just met us, and in this world, it's hard to trust anyone. How's 'bout we get to know each other over the stew and go from there."

The stew is little more than chunks of meat in a thin broth, but it's well-salted and has a hint of garlic to it and something else I can't quite place, which gives it a slightly smoky flavor. There's also the occasional kernel of field corn Scruff gleaned during his travels.

"Had it pretty good," Scruff says around a mouthful of soup. "Made my way out of town—I was working in San Antone—after things went to . . . uh . . . " He looks at the children. "After things went to blazes. Had me an old Toyota and ran 'er till I couldn't find fuel. Then that pulse thing hit—truck would've been useless anyway. Been on foot since then."

"Have you had any trouble with people?" Rey asks.

"Here and there. Mostly, I try to be a ghost. Sneaking around seems to keep me alive. Met up with John, and we've been stickin' with the same plan." He motions to his friend, who's so focused on his bowl he doesn't even notice. "Speaking of, all y'all might as well paint a target on your back with that horse and buggy."

"It's a wagon," Leanne snaps.

"More of a sleigh at the moment." Rochelle smiles.

"Call it what you wish." Scruff lifts his hands. "I'm telling ya, it's trouble. Them horses are gonna attract enough attention, but at least riding 'em you'd have speed on your side. Not so with your *wagon*."

"We've considered that," PJ says. "We thought we'd try and avoid more populated areas."

"Going to be hard in parts of Montana. Wyomin's been nice. Everything's spread out, making it fairly easy to sneak around towns. But looks like the advantage is comin' to an end. My map shows Montana isn't going to be so stealth. Not far across the state line there's a little town straddling the highway."

"Why'd you stop in Bakerville?" I ask.

"Saw a storm comin' in. Figured we needed to find a place to hole up, and the map said there was a town here. Turns out it's not much of a town. Y'all are the first people we've seen since we got here."

"Why are you using the community center? Why not one of the houses?"

"Couple reasons. Houses are sometimes . . . occupied, if'n you know what I mean."

Leanne scoffs while the rest of the adults say they do.

I glance at Debbie, who doesn't seem to be paying attention and is instead focused on her stew.

Leanne's son, Sebastian, drops his shoulders. I don't know the exact details of what he, his mom, and older sister experienced, but I've heard snippets. They walked from Oregon, arriving on the mountain only a month ago. A shiver runs through me as I think of the things Sebastian may have seen on their journey.

"Plus, the community center was listed on the map," Scruff says. "Figured, in this barren land, it gave me someplace to aim for and maybe, with it not being someone's private property, less chance of getting shot."

"So, you don't go into empty houses?" Sebastian asks.

"Now I didn't say that. I know there's benefits to empty houses. They've kept me alive."

"Yeah." Sebastian nods. "We found— "

"Enough, Sebastian," Leanne admonishes. "He doesn't need to know your business."

"The stew's good," Rochelle compliments. "Thank you for sharing with us."

"Got that old buck right on the creek a few days ago. Set up a nice fire to dry most of the meat. Cut and froze some too. John and me, we'd be happy to share with you folks, not only tonight but on the road. Got a little other food too. And both a rifle and shotgun for takin' more game."

"We don't eat deer on the mountain because it might have disease," Debbie says.

"Something wrong with the deer here?" Scruff asks.

PJ clears his throat. "Chronic Wasting Disease has been a problem in parts of Wyoming the last several years. It made some people leery of eating the meat."

"Chronic Wasting Disease." Scruff nods slowly. "Seems I may've heard of that. Never paid it no mind."

I smile around my mouthful of food. Both Dallas and Jackson were deer hunters, and both thought the whole CWD thing was nothing but a blown out of proportion farce brought on by anti-hunters. Of course, the two of them hunted together and shared many opinions about lots of things—pretty normal for brothers.

But as PJ said, some people are leery of eating the meat. Living on the mountain, the hunting crew only harvested elk or the occasional bighorn sheep or moose—no deer. However, if someone wanted to hunt on their own, they were allowed to do so. Which is exactly what PJ and Rochelle did when preparing for this trip. The two deer they harvested are an important part of our provisions.

When Jackson was still alive, he once borrowed a crossbow from the armory and brought a deer home for us. I spent days drying it over the community firepit and cooking the meat. We also kept some of the raw meat in a cooler buried in a snowbank behind the cabin. We had to be quiet about our cooler, though, since the community would've had a fit about food being left outside overnight.

We could get away with it during the daytime, like we did when processing the deer for this trip, but there were too many predators to risk it overnight: mountain lions, wolves, black bears, and grizzly bears. Predators don't limit their range to the mountain.

Bakerville and the river area has its share of them, and around my folks' house in Joliet too. Not the bears so much at their place but mountain lions and wolves. There was even a huge wolf killed outside of Joliet a few years ago.

Whew. What an uproar. While I hate that the animal was killed, I also understand why it happened. Dallas and Jackson, though, both got a laugh out of it and kept saying, "Smoke a pack a day! That'll take care of those elk-killing monsters." Both were convinced the elk population was declining as the wolf population increased.

I'm not so sure. But I do know my dad saw the wolf pack last spring before the terrorist attacks started. He even said the alpha is bigger than the one taken before.

"You folks said you've been living in the mountains? Seems it'd be a smart place to spend the winter. Why din't you wait until spring 'fore you gone traipsin' 'round the country?"

"We waited as long as we felt prudent," PJ says. "Besides, if you look at the calendar, spring's only about a week away."

"Today's March 16th." Kimba smiles.

"Don't that beat all." Scruff laughs. "I haven't looked at a calendar in a coon's age, but no way spring is anytime soon. Shoot, the cold last week about froze my . . . never mind 'bout that."

"Yeah," PJ agrees. "We thought we were going to have to postpone. But it's warmed up enough we figure we can travel on good days and hunker down when needed."

"Cold's not the only reason to hunker down. There's plenty of people out there with bad intentions. Evil. I wasn't joshin' all y'all 'bout the wagon. It's a risk."

PJ leans back in his chair and crosses his arms. "We have a plan. We won't take unnecessary chances."

Chapter 9

Scruff and John leave shortly after we finish eating. Rey, still using his American voice, tells them we'll discuss traveling together and give them our decision in the morning. Just in case, they should be ready to leave at dawn.

As soon as they're gone, PJ says, "Better get the rifles and handguns cleaned. The snow today didn't do them any favors. It's nice and dry in here with the fire, so let's take advantage of it."

To prevent all the guns from being torn apart at one time, PJ has half of us start with our rifles and the other half with pistols, except for Victoria Dawson's boys who keep watch while we clean and then they'll swap out with someone else so they can do their weapons.

Icky Vicky goes with her younger son, saying she'll keep him company. She's the only person over the age of fourteen not armed. She declared she hates guns. Somehow, likely due to her deceased husband's influence, she wasn't part of the militia. Or maybe she couldn't pass the mandatory physical or mental requirements. I don't know. But she's adamant about not carrying a weapon.

Rey convinced her she at least needed a knife, not only for defensive reasons but because it's practical with all the camping we're doing. She even argued about that before eventually giving in.

Seriously, I don't see what the big deal is with carrying a knife, but part of me can understand her apprehension to firearms. I'd only shot a gun a few times until I married Dallas. Even though I grew up in Montana, and guns are a part of the culture, I wasn't interested. My dad, a firearms enthusiast, wanted to take me shooting, but I found them to be loud and scary. My mom, also not a gun fan, told him not to push me.

I was never really interested in most of the things small-town Montana girls were supposed to be interested in. All my friends loved hiking, hunting, horses, and the outdoors. Not me. I preferred to be inside reading or helping my mom in the kitchen. Or, even better, our twice-yearly trips to Denver for shopping.

One time, Mom even took me to Seattle! She'd grown up on the East Coast and, although she loved Joliet in some ways, she missed the city life. She even encouraged me to move to Denver after I finished college. I was there about eighteen months before I met Dallas through a friend of a friend and we started long-distance dating.

Dallas was the quintessential Wyoming boy. He and Jackson grew up in a small town on the Wyoming and South Dakota border, doing all the things country boys did: riding motorcycles, driving pickup trucks through the mud, shooting guns, and more.

At first, our time together was limited with him visiting me in the city or me going to his place. Sometimes, we'd meet halfway for a weekend. During that time, he didn't push me to do the outdoorsy stuff. But after we moved in together, he thought I'd enjoy that life too. I didn't.

The first few months were a struggle as we worked to find a balance between our individual interests. It wasn't really until we were married and living in Prospect that we found a happy medium.

He did help me become comfortable with firearms, and I got to the point I could go out plinking with him or shooting targets. That was fine, but it wasn't something I wanted to spend a lot of time on. And I certainly did learn firearms are a useful tool. I know that now more than ever. I also understand the importance of caring for them.

I'm with Kimba and a couple of others, using the coffee table in the living room to clean our pistols. Those cleaning rifles are at the dining room table and the folding table PJ set up.

My pistol, an American-made compact 9-millimeter from FNS, was a gift from Dallas—our tenth anniversary gift, in fact. At the time, I wasn't too happy to receive it. I'd wanted a diamond anniversary band. I'd not only dropped hints about wanting it, but I also flat out told him that was what I expected to receive. He'd also dropped a few hints, but I didn't pick up what he was putting down.

We'd met up with Jackson to go sight in a new handgun he'd just bought. Dallas kept saying how he thought I'd enjoy a similar one of my own. He and Jackson both hounded me to shoot the new gun. While it was fine and was even fun to shoot, I had no desire to have one of my own. Why would I even want a gun? It's not like I'd ever use it or find joy in it. Not like a diamond band, which I'd love every time I looked at it and saw it sparkling on my finger.

I didn't even try to hide my disappointment over the gift. In the years since I received the 9-millimeter, I'd only shot it twice until getting ready for this trip. And I never did get the anniversary band. I let out a quiet snort. Good thing. The pistol is certainly more useful in today's world than a ring would be.

Although I now carry my handgun on my hip, I'm still not overly comfortable with it. I'm awkward and keep thinking it's in my way. I've been practicing with it and have come a long way in the few weeks since I began my training, but I'll never be as self-assured as Kimba is with her weapons. Not even as confident as Rochelle. I'd like to think I'll do what I need to do, though, especially if it involves keeping my children safe.

Before any of us take our weapons apart, PJ gathers all the magazines and extra rounds. "The master bathroom counter is good sized. I'll put the ammunition in there. If you still have ammo in your backpacks, move them to your sleeping room. No ammunition in the kitchen or living room while we're cleaning."

I resist rolling my eyes over the ridiculousness of the no-ammo rule. When we had a meeting in preparation of leaving, he told us about this. He made a point of telling Rey they can do whatever they wish after the group breaks apart, but up until then, this gun-safety rule is nonnegotiable. After the meeting, I asked Rochelle if PJ is always so intense. She said he's just careful. He had a friend from college who died in what was determined to be an accidental discharge.

"Hey, Rey." Donnie McCullough looks up from his seat at the folding table where's he's field stripping his rifle. "What's with the accent, man?"

Rey and Kimba both let out a low laugh.

"My daddy does that sometimes," their youngest daughter says from her spot near the woodstove. "He likes people to think he's a normal American."

"Is that something left over from your spy days?" Donnie asks.

"Something like that, mate," Rey answers in his normal accented voice. "I'll come clean with Scruff and John if they join us."

"You'll need to." PJ nods. "My guess is Scruff doesn't miss much. He'll wonder why you were faking. But John . . . I'm not sure if he cares what's happening one way or another."

"What do you all think?" Rey asks.

"Where exactly are they going?" I ask.

"I don't even think they know." Kimba looks up from her weapon. She motions to her husband. "Can you hand me another swab? I may have fudged a bit in sharing our plans with Scruff and John. They don't know exactly where we're going, just the general direction."

"Two more mouths to feed is the last thing we need." Leanne shakes her head.

"They'll bring food with them," PJ says. "And Scruff has been surviving on his own for a while. He doesn't even look too bad."

"Is that supposed to be some kind of an insult?" Leanne glares at him.

"Not at all," PJ answers. "It's a statement expressing he isn't going hungry. Leads me to believe he'd be more of an asset than a hindrance. John looks okay too. Truth is, I doubt they need us. They're probably just looking for company—especially Scruff. He's a talker, and it doesn't seem like John participates much."

"Why bother?" I ask. "Scruff made it sound like they have things to their advantage. What'd he say? He's a ghost?"

"It's probably quite the advantage," Donnie agrees. "When my brother and I were riding around trying to find someone to help in our fight against Richard Majors and his henchmen in Prospect, stealth was our friend too."

The room goes quiet for several beats at the mention of Richard Majors. I glance to Robyn as she wipes at her eye. Majors was behind the massacre of her husband and the others who stayed in Bakerville proper.

"'Course," Donnie says, "Scruff wearing a bright red jumpsuit doesn't make him seem too stealthy."

"Definitely doesn't," Rey agrees. "But against the white of the snow, our muted clothes stick out too. We probably should've taken Leanne's friend's advice and made white suits to go over the top."

"Clarice is not my friend," Leanne scoffs.

"She's my friend," Leanne's son says defiantly. "And she's Mr. Ben's wife."

That was another juicy bit of gossip from the kitchen crew. Leanne and her children showed up last month at the ski lodge along with another couple and several children. Seems Leanne had traveled with the husband but not with the wife and other children. It also seems Leanne thought the wife was dead and she'd be the next missus.

From the buzz I heard, it makes me wonder if her bitterness and insistence on leaving were related to thinking she was jilted. Or maybe she was like me and just couldn't handle being the focus of scandal day in and day out. Of course, it's not like she really did anything to become the center of attention, other than being unpleasant to people. It's not like her husband was a known killer or something.

I heard about her situation while peeling sugar beets and chopping meat, but listen was all I did. She may have been the newest community outcast, but I'd long been persona non grata. I'd show up and do my work, listening but never contributing to any conversation. No matter which duty crew I was on, it was always the same thing: side glances and evil eyes. While everyone else talked and carried on, I kept my head down and my ears open.

Sure, I could've argued, could've defended myself. But I'd felt so defeated—beaten even. Why bother? I barely had the energy to get through each day. Why argue with people whose minds were already made up?

The smell of gun oil wafts through the room. I close my eyes and inhale the scent. Dallas used to tease that I should put a little drop of his favorite brand behind each ear. He said the orange bottle of gun oil would make the best perfume ever. I release a long, slow breath before opening my eyes.

Leanne, at the end of the folding table, has her tongue sticking out the side of her mouth as she works on her rifle. Donnie motions toward the weapon, asking her if she needs any help. She snorts and shakes her head, throwing him the evil eye for good measure.

She's really a miserable person.

I'm glad I don't have to be around her for any more than a few days. I don't know how the others are going to be able to put up with her with the distances they have ahead of them. I'm sure Leanne will make every step miserable. She's such an obnoxious person, positively loathsome. *Loathsome Leanne.* It's the perfect name for her.

The group had originally planned to split in Joliet, but adding Loathsome Leanne and her children brought up new route options. She's going to a relative's home in Lewistown, Montana. Even though it's out of the way from the original plans, Lewistown is on an alternate road to Great Falls.

So now, after leaving me in Joliet, the plan is everyone will stay together and take Robyn to her folks' house outside of Billings before continuing to the summer camp where Rochelle's son was last summer when the world fell apart. Once they find Christopher,

Rochelle and PJ will return to Bakerville, and the rest of the group will continue on foot to Lewistown and then Great Falls.

I try not to worry about Rochelle, worry about what she might find at the camp. I've held her hand a few times while she prayed for her son. It seems to help her feel better. I'm not sure how much good praying will really do, but I figure it can't really hurt. I can't even imagine how I'd feel if one of my children was not with me during this terrible time. With so much danger around, is her son safe? Is he even alive?

"Do you think he'll be able to keep up?" Beth asks. "Scruff seems pretty old."

"Beth!" I chastise.

"Well, he is," she mumbles.

"He's not too old." A slight smile plays on PJ's face. "And he looks plenty fit."

"It'd probably be a whole lot easier on him, on all of us, if we weren't going out of our way to take her home," Leanne says, pointing her bony finger in my direction.

"We've discussed this, Leanne." Rochelle's voice is soft and kind.

"Discussed? I don't think so. You all made your decision and don't give a lick about my opinion on the matter. It's clear when looking at a map that Joliet is out of our way."

Just like always, she says Joliet wrong. She pronounces it Joe-lee-ett, like the town in Illinois. Those of us from around here know it's Jah-lee-ett. I corrected her the first time she said it wrong. The tongue-lashing I received made it not worth correcting her again.

"We're going to make sure Tamra and her children get home," PJ says. "We listened to your thoughts on the matter."

"Oh, I know. You've made it quite clear my opinion, and the fact we're adding more than twenty miles and several days to the trip, doesn't count for diddly squat. I still say she and her girls will be fine if they cut off and head west so we can continue on our way without taking a ridiculous detour."

"Not happening, Leanne." Kimba gives her a pointed look. "Now, back to the discussion at hand, which is Scruff."

Leanne rolls her eyes and shakes her head. "Do you care about my opinion regarding him? Doubtful."

Kimba's bright blue eyes bore into Leanne. Her mouth tilts in a slight smile. "We'll discuss and then vote. Majority rules."

Ignoring the stare, Leanne asks, "What if it doesn't work out? What then?"

"He doesn't strike me as one who'd hold a grudge," Kimba says evenly. "My guess is, if it doesn't work out, he'll tell us goodbye like a gentleman and be on his way. John will probably go along with whatever Scruff decides."

"I agree," Jennifer Dosen adds. "Scruff seems very secure, the type who follows the Golden Rule."

Jennifer has mentioned the Golden Rule several times during our planning for the trip and even the short time we've been on the road. It seems she thinks it's important to live in a manner of treating others how you'd like to be treated. She even goes out of her way to be kind to Leanne, who, as far as I'm concerned, deserves no kindness at all.

As if to punctuate my thought of what Leanne does and doesn't deserve, she responds in her typical fashion. "Humph." She flips her wild mane, giving Jennifer the stink eye. "You and your Golden Rule nonsense. That may have been something in the Podunk town you lived in, but we're in the real world now, in the middle of a disaster. There's no place in this world for such nonsense. It's more like do unto others *before* they do unto you."

Jennifer gives a slight shake of her head along with a small smile. "There's always a place for treating people kindly."

Kindly, sure. But Jennifer is really excessive about it. She goes out of her way to smile and help people, which is fine. I'm not against being polite, but she takes it to the extreme, even forgiving people who don't deserve it, like Victoria Dawson. I'll never understand how she's able to forgive her, to even be friends with her again, after what happened.

I mean, sure, Icky Vicky didn't pull the trigger of the gun that killed Jennifer's sister, and she wasn't directly involved in the attempted insurrection . . . but still. It's amazing to me Jennifer is so easy to forgive. I mean, I wouldn't expect a family of someone Jackson wronged to forgive me.

Wronged.

What a paltry way to think of the terrible things Jackson did.

"I think Leanne's right," the youngest of the two Dawson boys says. "That Scruff—he has shifty eyes. We probably shouldn't trust him."

"Shifty eyes?" Kimba asks. "Scruff has a scar near the one eye. It looks pretty recent. I don't think that makes his eyes shifty."

"Well, whatever it is, I don't like it. I don't think we should trust him. He's probably trouble. And the other one, he's too quiet. We shouldn't trust him either."

"He's just sad," Debbie says. "He looks very, very sad."

"We're all sad. But he doesn't have to mope around and act all . . . all weird."

"Okay, so when we take a vote, you can vote against them joining us," PJ says.

"I want to check in with the guys on watch, see what they think." Rey scoots his chair from the table. "Then, unless we need more discussion, I think we should vote."

Surprisingly, the only no votes were Jameson Dawson, Leanne, and me. Even the younger children voted for inviting Scruff and John to join us. I do believe, had the children's votes swayed the final tally, there would've been an adult-only recount.

Truthfully, I don't like the fact I seem to have aligned myself with Leanne. Her excessive anger isn't something I want in my life, and voting the same as she did seems like I may be ushering that in.

Of course, her animosity for me doesn't fade with our matching vote. As the group breaks up, she shoots me a dirty look. "I hope you're happy about causing unneeded risk because you're too big of a baby to spend a few days on your own."

She's not wrong. I have no desire to be out in the world with only my girls. That'd be stupid.

Chapter 10

With the vote to include Scruff and John in our group finished and the guns cleaned, I take my girls into the master bedroom where we're staying tonight—not just us but Rochelle, Robyn, Jennifer, and Victoria also. While I'm not overly pleased with so many roommates, at least Leanne isn't one of them. Victoria Dawson is bad enough.

I have no desire to share a room with her. I don't think of her as Icky Vicky just to be mean. She smells bad. In all fairness, with the days of easy showering gone, I'm sure we all smell. But not like her. When I first met her last fall, she was what Dallas would've called a debutante. The world had gone nuts several months earlier, and she still wore makeup and nail polish. Seriously? Who cares about that stuff when day-to-day living's a struggle?

Now she's a disheveled mess. She doesn't even try to make herself presentable. It's so bad her hair is matted, and her stench—ugh. Her change in grooming habits occurred around the time her husband attempted to usurp the legitimate government on the mountain. That's when he killed Jennifer Dosen's sister and several others. He, along with most of his coconspirators, were also killed in the process.

Victoria insists her husband had gone crazy. The stress of the apocalypse and wanting to help the community to not only survive but to thrive got to him, and he snapped. Snapped to the point he and his cronies took several children hostage during the attempted coup d'état.

While neither Beth nor Debbie were part of the children taken hostage, they were standing nearby when the shooting began. There was no warning either. People were laughing and having a great time at the wedding reception of fellow townspeople. The food service had just begun when *bam*! There was sudden chaos with gunfire and screaming.

My girls and Rochelle's had already gone up to fill their plates, while she and I stood talking. When the shooting started, I tried to run toward them, but in the chaos, I was tripped. From where I was sprawled on the floor, I couldn't even see what was happening. It was maddening and was a few of the longest—and scariest—minutes of my life. When it was finished, almost a dozen were dead.

I'm sure a good amount of Victoria's current condition stems from that. Part of me thinks I should be more understanding, be forgiving and benevolent like Jennifer. I mean, it's not like Victoria's husband is the only one who did terrible things. I've thought about trying to befriend her. Maybe I would if she hadn't been one of the people who made a point of putting their hands in front of their mouths to talk about me as I'd walk by.

Before she became an outcast herself, she had plenty of so-called friends and seemed to go out of her way to make rude comments about others. She'd done the same to Rochelle when the news of her situation first came out. I'd heard her talk about Kimba, sharing some totally wild stories about the terrible things Kimba did during her time as a government operative—as a spy or whatever she really was. I even heard her call Jennifer things like pious and preachy, and that was when they were supposed to be friends, long before her crazy husband killed Jennifer's sister.

Icky Vicky. It's a perfectly fitting name when combining her terrible hygiene with her behavior. When I first met her, she didn't even have an accent! She pretended to be a regular Wyoming gal, not from some Appalachian backcountry or wherever it is she's from. Appearances were everything to her and her crazy husband. But since he died, she doesn't bother hiding the country bumpkin twang any more than she bothers with combing her hair.

"It's still cold in here, Mommy," Debbie says.

"We'll set your tent up. That'll help keep you warm."

"You'll get in with us? After you finish your job?"

"I'll come in here to sleep when I'm finished with sentry duty, but I'll let you and Beth have the tent. I'll make my own cozy little space. Okay?"

She pulls me into a hug. "Be careful."

Once the room is set up, I give both girls a goodnight kiss before following Rochelle to the living room. She's also on first watch.

"Ready, Tamra?" Rey asks.

"Yep." I look around the living room. "Will we both be in here?"

Rochelle scrunches up her face. "One of us inside and the other outside. Then we'll switch."

"Outside? In the . . . in the snow?"

"You want to flip for which one you'll do first?" PJ asks, his mustache twitching in amusement.

"No, that's fine. I'll go outside first. Is that okay?"

"Sure." Rochelle shrugs.

"I, um, I know we went over how sentry duty would work when we were having our meetings to get ready, but I've never done this before. Can you tell me again what to do?"

"There's not much to it," PJ says. "Stay awake and stay alert."

"This is a walking sentry duty," Rey adds. "You're going to be tempted to keep repeating the same path over and over, but it's best if you alter it. Go around the backside, then the frontside. Mix it up."

"You can wear my cleats," Rochelle offers. "They'll be easier for walking in than those ski contraptions."

"There's too much snow for those." PJ shakes his head. "They're best for keeping you from slipping on the ice. Better give her your snowshoes."

"Thanks, that'll help," I say with a nod.

Although the bulk of us are on skis, PJ, Donnie, and Rochelle have snowshoes. They are their own personal items, brought with them to the mountain. Well, not Rochelle. She didn't own anything when she went up to the mountain, but PJ's family had a pair they gave her. PJ and Rochelle also each have a pair of chain and spike contraptions.

Donnie was a recent addition to the mountain community, having been a friend of PJ's family. His horse and belongings are his and his alone since the rules of *contribution to the good of society* were lifted after Icky Vicky's husband attempted the coup. The three of them don't walk, since Donnie rides his horse and PJ and Rochelle sit on the wagon bench, but the snowshoes proved useful last night for sentry duty and getting around camp.

"You won't be able to see much distance," PJ says. "As overcast as it is, the moon isn't going to be much help. You're not relying on sight but listening for anything out of the ordinary."

"And if I hear something?"

"Let Rochelle know. If you think there's someone close and they'll hear you, click the radio twice. Otherwise, just tell her what's going on."

"I still can't believe you were able to bring these." I take the walkie-talkie PJ hands me.

"The radios weren't that big of a deal. The batteries, though, those were the challenge."

"Good thing your dad's girlfriend told you about her cache." Rey smacks PJ lightly on the shoulder.

When we arrived at this house, PJ made a point of going to the barn where the homeowner had stashed a few things she didn't want to take up the mountain. She gave PJ permission to use anything we thought we'd need.

"Yep," PJ says. "My guess is she's not the only one who set aside a few things for when they returned from their winter of communal living."

"How about you?" I ask.

He gives a slight bend of his neck. "We stowed a few things before we blew our house up."

"That must've been hard," Rey says. "It was the right thing to do, though."

I look at my boots, not the uncomfortable backcountry ski boots but regular snow boots. Thanks to the wagon, we were all able to bring a few extra things: a second pair of boots, athletic shoes, and a few other essentials. The well-packed wagon is in the barn, where the contents have been rearranged after adding the goods PJ's friend told him about.

There's even several bales of hay and a bag of oats. We left the mountain with some food for the horses, but not nearly enough for the entire trip. Even with the addition from the barn, they'll still need to find more. As it is, the wagon's loaded as full as PJ feels prudent for the horses not to struggle.

I expected Leanne to balk at the additional items being put in the wagon, changing their seating arrangements and making it even tighter than it was. She was surprisingly agreeable, suggesting the hay might help keep them warm and would provide a barricade if someone started shooting.

Tuning back into PJ's talk about ruining his home outside of Prospect when Majors's group took over the town—the same group that killed the people living in Bakerville—I wonder about my own home within the Prospect city limits. I left there before the EMP and before Richard Majors's rise to power. We didn't even know anything about Majors until PJ and his family rode into Bakerville around the same time we were moving to the mountain for winter.

"Do you think . . . there shouldn't be anyone around here, right?" I ask.

"You mean other than Scruff and John? I don't think so," Rey answers. "We didn't see any other tracks, and they haven't seen anyone since arriving."

"The Prospect people . . . they won't come back?"

"Doubtful. They did what they set out to do—kill just about everyone. It's unlikely they'd return."

"It's more likely they'll start planning how to go after our friends and family at the ski lodge." PJ scratches his bearded chin.

"I don't believe they'll plan an invasion until the weather breaks," Rey says.

"Why not? They attacked here in February," I say, moving my hand around to encompass the winter wonderland we're still engulfed in.

"Yes, it's true." Rey sighs. "But there's considerably more snow at the ski lodge than at this lower elevation. They know about the weather. It'd make sense to wait. Besides, we don't know for sure if they even know about our move to the mountain."

"Do you really believe that?" PJ asks. "My guess is they know full well where everyone went. And part of me really hates that I've left my friends and family behind when they could be in danger."

"Why did you?" I ask, quickly regretting my question as I watch Rochelle's eyes fill with tears. "I mean, I know why you did. You know, so you could help— "

"I made a commitment to Rochelle. I'm a man of my word."

"Believe me, we've talked about it many times." Rochelle's voice is low. "After the massacres, we both knew the rest of our people could be targets. You and I have talked about it, too, Tamra. I gave PJ an out, told him I understood— "

"Like I said," PJ interrupts, "I gave Rochelle my word. And with spring on the horizon, or so we hope, now was the time to leave."

"None of us feel overly good about going when our friends and family may be in danger," Rey says. "But just like PJ, Kimba and I promised the Dosens we'd help them get home. Sometimes we have to do things even when we don't want to, even when it's dangerous."

"I'd like to think we prayed over this and are doing what we feel God led us to do." PJ looks to Rochelle, who gives a nod.

I resist the urge to shake my head. I'll never understand how they think praying about something is going to give them answers. Do they really believe God speaks to them? Or that He'll provide some kind of divine intervention if they beg enough?

"Amen, brother." Rey claps PJ on the shoulder again. "Anyway, Tamra. Questions?"

"Um, can I use my flashlight?"

"It's best if you can do without, but if you need it, keep it low. You'll ruin your night vision every time you turn it on."

"Okay, I'll try."

"Right, then. You'll have the first half of your watch outside. Walk like we've talked, go inside the barn to warm up—there's a chair in there. Have a seat if you want, but don't get too comfortable. You're outside for the first hour and a half, then you and Rochell will switch. When you're inside, go from the front of the house to the back, looking out the windows. Again, you're mainly listening—especially for Rochelle to tell you she has a problem. Got it?"

"Got it."

"It'll be more difficult to stay awake inside." Rey gives me a serious look. "You'll be inside, out of the cold. It might be tempting to sit down and close your eyes a minute— "

"I won't."

"If it keeps snowing like this, we'll need to wait it out," PJ says. "Might not be able to leave tomorrow."

My body gives an involuntary shudder just thinking of the cold. "Especially with the wind. It could get too cold to be outside for long."

"If it picks up, make your routes short. Don't risk frostbite, okay?"

"Yep. Okay."

"Then we'll leave you to it," Rey says. "You want one of us to walk you out?"

"No need." I start putting on my cold-weather gear.

"We should pray first." Rochelle reaches for my hand.

"Do you usually pray before taking a watch shift?" I ask.

"Well, not always, but . . . it feels right, like we should."

"Okay." I give her a patient smile, releasing her gentle grip. "You go ahead if you want, but I'm going to finish getting ready."

I pull on my dark orange stocking cap, making sure it goes low enough to cover my ears, then add an insanely ugly dark yellow plaid scarf over the top of an almost as ugly red plaid gaiter. My uncoordinated ensemble does little to complement my dark gray heavy coat, but at least I'm warm.

PJ touches Rochelle's shoulder. "Robyn and Jennifer have watch after you two. Wake them when it's time."

"Uh, I don't have a watch."

"I gave my watch to Rochelle. Keep your collar pulled up. Remember, step inside the barn as you need to."

A couple of minutes later, as I walk out the back door, I not only pull my collar up but also pull up my gaiter, wrap my scarf a little tighter, and pull my stocking cap down. I take a leisurely lap around the property. I'm less than halfway when the snow really starts coming down, not big fluffy pretty flakes but tiny wet ones. If it were daylight, there'd probably be zero visibility. If it were slightly warmer, it'd probably be sleet. And if this keeps up, I'm going to be a wet, soggy mess by the time my outside watch is over. And there'll be no way to leave tomorrow. We'll be stuck here until the weather clears.

With the wind and the snow, walking is less than comfortable. On my first pass around the house, I tangle my snowshoes and go down. So much for these being easier. One round is all I can handle before needing to go in the barn and warm up. Instead of sitting on the chair, I lean against the doorframe, somewhat sheltered from the wind and out of the driving snow, shivering to keep myself warm.

I wish Dallas was here. Nights always seem to be the hardest for me, when I miss him the most. That and first thing in the morning when I wake up and realize he's not next to me. I now realize that rushing into the marriage with Jackson was my attempt to keep Dallas alive. Being brothers, they were similar. Or so I thought.

After my shaking mostly subsides, I start another loop. This time I go through the front yard first, loop around the house, and warm up, then repeat the process a few more times. Surely, I must be close to the end of my hour and a half outside. The snow's letting up slightly, but the wind has picked up. It's going to be completely miserable for Rochelle. I take a deep breath and start a new circle.

I'm halfway between the barn and the front yard when a gunshot cuts through the night. I grab the walkie-talkie off my belt, fumbling it between both hands before dropping it in the snow. I fish the small flashlight out of my pocket, desperately moving the beam around until I spot the radio.

I quickly wipe some of the snow off the radio before clicking the button to talk. "Someone's shooting. I don't . . . I'm not sure what's happening. We may be under attack."

"Copy that." Rochelle sounds completely calm.

"What do I do?" I ask, the panic evident in my voice.

"Wait one."

My heart is pounding. I stay kneeling, waiting for more shooting and instructions from Rochelle.

I'm just about ready to click the radio again when Rochelle finally comes back on. "If you're not at the chair, return there. Backup's on the way."

I scramble up from the ground, tripping over one of the snowshoes and unhooking it. Instead of taking the time to put it back on, I grab it, running with one on and one off. I'm a few yards from the door when my booted foot catches on something and I go down. "C'mon!" I cry out as I awkwardly get back on my feet.

Stepping inside the building, I move to the chair. I'm too scared to sit, so I stand in front of it, leaving the door open as I pant to catch my breath.

Within a minute, a low voice says, "Tamra, it's Rey. I'm coming in the door."

"Yeah, okay."

"Can you holster your weapon for me?"

"I don't . . . it's not out." I feel like an idiot. I didn't even think to pull my pistol or move the rifle to firing position.

"Okay, then. Coming in."

"Rey!" I rush to him as soon as he steps in the barn. "There was a shot. I don't know where."

"Just the one?"

"I think so."

"All right. You're with me. Brett, c'mon in here and stand watch from the barn."

"Yes, sir," the older of Icky Vicky Dawson's boys says as he steps inside.

"Let's go, Tamra. Atticus and his brothers have the perimeter. We'll meet up with Kimba and PJ. The rest have the house. I'll take the radio."

My hands are still shaking as I hand it off to him. "Let me put the snowshoe back on." I take a deep breath as I work the buckle with my trembling fingers.

"Any idea where the shot originated?" Rey asks before we step out of the barn.

"I don't know."

"Where were you when you heard it?"

"I was taking another loop, heading toward the front."

"Okay, let's go then. When we get to where you were, stop me."

As we walk out of the building, I realize I'm not wearing my gloves. I must have removed them when I was trying to work the radio. I shove my hands deep in my pockets.

"Anything?" Kimba asks as she appears in the dark with PJ by her side.

"Nothing new," Rey answers.

"You think it came from the community center?" PJ asks.

"It could have." I nod. "Do you think they're under attack?"

"One shot, you said?" PJ asks.

"Just the one."

"Let's head that way." Kimba motions with her head. "You take the lead. Tamra and I will stay behind you."

"Um . . . I could stay here."

"It's best you stay with us," Rey says. "Stick by Kimba."

A gust of wind hits me hard as we begin to cross the road. I'm recovering my footing when Kimba puts out her arm. "Hold it, Tamra."

"Is that you, Scruff?" Rey calls out.

"Yeah, it's me," he yells over the wind. "There's no threat."

"Let's catch up with them." Kimba urges me forward.

"Everything okay?" Rey asks.

We're only a few feet from the men, but it's still hard to hear over the roar of the wind.

"Thought y'all might've heard the shot." Scruff's voice is hoarse. "Was headin' your way to tell ya not to worry."

"And?" Kimba asks.

"It's John. Things must've been— " He lets out a sigh. "Guess it got to be too much for him."

Chapter 11

After we help move John's body to a storage shed, PJ puts a hand on Scruff's shoulder. "I'll leave a note at the house we're staying in. They'll see it and take care of him, give him a proper burial when the ground thaws."

"Appreciate it," Scruff says. "He was a good man. Quiet and haunted. But good. Lost his family only days before he and I met up. Just couldn't seem to shake the grief. I'd like to . . . to have moment with him."

While Scruff says goodbye to his friend, Rey calls on the radio to let Rochelle know it's all clear and everyone could stand down. He also asks for her to find someone else to cover the rest of my shift.

We stay with Scruff for several hours, first helping him clean the community center bathroom where John had taken his life and then just listening as he talks and reminisces about the friend he'd been traveling with for the last several months.

We invite him to stay in the house with us, but he says he's fine and would rather be alone for now.

"I'd still like to travel with you if'n you're willin'," he says.

"That'll be fine." Rey answers, letting a little of his British slip. "I don't think we'll be leaving anytime soon, though. Taking a day off and letting the storm pass, that'll be best."

~~~~~

The weather caused us a two-day delay in Bakerville. There was lots of grumbling, but it was just too windy and wet to risk leaving the house. During the daylight, I spent hours looking for my gloves in the snow and still only found one. I have a second pair, but they aren't nearly as warm as the ones I was wearing. I'm completely irritated at myself for dropping them—so irritated that I actually started to cry. It's ridiculous to cry over a missing glove.

While I was looking for my glove, Kimba sought me out. "You doing okay?" she asked.

"Just looking for the glove I dropped."
~~~~~

"Let me help. We can talk a little at the same time."

"About?"

"Rey said you still had your pistol holstered when he reached you last night. Did you draw it at all?"

"I . . . no. I didn't even think of it until Rey asked about it."

"It's hard to get used to when you're new to carrying. And it's hard to know how to react in different circumstances. I know PJ spent some time trying to get you comfortable with your weapons before we left. You're not the only one who isn't fully confident. Even those in the militia didn't have as much training over the winter as we did last summer. Your reaction reminded us that we need to be training again, get everyone crisp and self-confident so they can improve their reaction times."

That afternoon we started working on different drills with the unloaded pistols, including learning to draw. After that, we moved on to training with the rifles and then did some martial arts stuff.

I liked it but quickly realized Kimba was downplaying the rest of the group's skills. They were all much better than me. Except Icky Vicky. She refused to participate in any of it and just stayed in the house while we did our stuff in the garage.

Even Scruff joined us. It was apparent the death of his friend weighed heavy on him, but he was still a welcome addition to the group. Although he didn't stay with us the first time we asked, after we finished the training exercises, he moved into the barn and asked to be put on the watch schedule. He seems to fit in effortlessly.

And I was wrong about him. His age isn't a hindrance to our traveling. If anything, he's a faster snowshoer than I am a skinner. We left the house in Bakerville this morning, and it's been a long, full day of breaking snow.

"Is it much farther?" Beth asks from behind me.

"To the state line? We should see it anytime," I say.

Not a minute later, someone near the front of the line calls out, "There it is!"

We're suddenly moving faster, anticipating crossing over from Wyoming into Montana. Even though the land looks the same—flat with mountains in the distance, the same mountains we used to live in—I feel like we're getting somewhere.

The smile on my face falters as the sign comes into view. Only part of it's intact; the rest is gone. Vandalized.

"Too bad." Jennifer shakes her head as she reaches for her water bottle.

"Looks like the other sign—the one going into Wyoming—is still there." One of Jennifer's boys points to the intact *Welcome to Wyoming* billboard.

"Are we stopping here?" Beth asks. "Camping, I mean."

"Maybe up a little farther," Kimba answers. "PJ knows this area, says there's some decent fields along the river. With all the geese we've been seeing, it might give us some good hunting."

We've chosen to travel the main highway, winding alongside the Clarks Fork of the Yellowstone River. And PJ's right, there are a lot of farms dotting the area along the highway and the river. Scruff's proficiency with a shotgun already came in handy when we stopped for a quick lunch and he brought down a couple of geese. And early this morning, one of Jennifer's boys harvested a rabbit.

PJ brings the wagon to a stop. He pumps a fist in the air. "Now we're getting somewhere!"

Our break is almost festive, with laughing and even a few jokes. Surprisingly, there's even something resembling a smile from Leanne when her son high-fives her. As we sip from our water bottles and gnaw on pieces of jerky, I drink in the beauty of the area. The mountains to the west with flat farmland are a sharp contrast to our immediate east with rolling hills and rock outcroppings. I've driven this road hundreds of times between my home in Prospect and my parents' place in Joliet. I still never tire of the landscape—such diversity!

"What do you think, PJ?" Rey asks. "Got a good camp spot in mind for us?"

"That or maybe a house. Let's get moving, travel an hour and then stop well before dark so we can set up. We'll sleep on the riverfront tonight."

"Wait." Rey holds his hand up in a fist. "Movement in the field."

I squint my eyes, trying to see what Rey saw.

"You sure?" Kimba asks, her voice quiet, her stance ready.

"More birds?" Scruff asks.

Rey gives a slow shake of his head. "I don't think so."

"Should we go check it out?" the oldest of the A Boys asks.

"Kimba, you get our group moving. Atticus and I will stay behind and follow the wagon."

"What do we do?" I ask, motioning Beth and Debbie to move behind the wagon.

"You and your daughters keep moving. The ones who are usually in the wagon, stay low. Everyone keep your head on a swivel."

I shake my head as tears sting my eyes. "You're going to have to talk plain and simple to me, not in your military mumbo jumbo."

"He just means to stay alert." Rochelle touches my arm.

"That's right." Rey's voice is slow and calm. "Stay alert and let's get moving. Rochelle, take the team. Um, you can drive it from the passenger's side, right?"

"The passenger's side?" she asks. "Uh, yeah."

"Hey," Rey says, his voice purposefully light. "I'm not exactly knowledgeable with those kinds of things."

"Should you be joking at a time like this?" I ask.

"It might seem like he's not taking this seriously," Kimba says, "but I promise you he's watching and aware of everything happening. Now let's get the children and Leanne in the wagon. Everyone else get your skis on and start moving. We're going to be okay, but we need to stay alert."

"I don't think they're gonna attack." Scruff's eyes are scanning the area. "Seems more like they're watching, waiting for us to leave—being cautious like."

With my heart pounding, I help Debbie into the wagon, cautioning her to keep her head down while she's getting in and seated.

Uncharacteristically, Leanne touches my arm. She gives me a slight nod. "I'll watch out for her."

Biting my lip to keep the threatening tears at bay, I respond with a nod.

Beth already has her skis on. I quickly move up where mine are laying in the snow and try to get my boots attached to the bindings. I'm shaking so hard, even my feet are trembling.

In a whisper, Beth says, "We're okay, Mom. Kimba and Rey—they know what to do. We just need to go."

With a snap, the boot finally falls into place.

Scruff motions for me and Beth to move in front of him. Within seconds, we're moving at a brisk pace. We keep up at an accelerated clip until the road bends and there's a hillside between us and the field Rey saw movement in. Once we're well around the corner, Kimba calls us to a halt as we wait for Rey and Atticus.

"What's keeping them?" one of the teenagers asks.

"They'll make sure we're not being followed," Kimba answers.

"Followed? We're on the highway." I motion to the snow-covered ground. "We're leaving tracks. They can easily catch up with us anytime."

"Yes, true," she answers. "I meant, not being followed right now."

It's several minutes before Rey and Atticus come around the bend, with Rey giving a thumbs up as soon as he sees us.

"Let's keep moving," he says when they're close enough they don't need to shout.

"Same speed?" Kimba asks.

"Normal speed. Can you keep the lead, love? Break the trail. Atticus and I will stay at the rear."

"Are they behind us?" I ask.

"Doesn't seem like it. We'll just keep on guard to make sure."

After what must have been close to an hour without stopping, based on how much the sun has dropped, Kimba finally calls for a halt. "There's a house up ahead. From here, I'd guess it's vacant."

I follow her finger to where she points at a moderate-sized ranch-style house.

"I'll be happy to check it out," Scruff says.

"Donnie?" Rey motions to the big man on his horse. "You up for helping him?"

"Yup. You ready, old timer?"

"We'll cover you," Rey says. He has all the children Beth's age and younger get in the wagon, then asks Rochelle to move it back to a bend in the road. She'll keep the team at the ready. Robyn and I are directed to stay with the wagon, as are the two teens with shotguns. "Let's get the wagon moved, then we'll get everyone else in position."

Rochelle slowly drives the wagon while the four of us walk alongside. Once we get in place, the rest move to their strategic positions while Donnie, on his horse, with Scruff walking beside him, move cautiously toward the house.

After many tense minutes, Donnie and Scruff finally reach the house. Leaving his horse near a tree, they move around the place, looking in windows and checking the outbuildings before disappearing around the back. A few minutes later, Donnie comes back out and waves his cowboy hat. Rey then waves us over to him.

"I guess that means everything is okay?" Robyn asks.

"Seems so." I cock my head to the side. "Good thing since it's going to be dark soon."

Inside the house, Scruff says, "All y'all will wanna stay out of the back bedroom. It's good we're here in the dead of winter and not the heat of summer. We put a sign on the door to show you which one. The rest of the house is fine. Even found a good stash of firewood. Soon as it's dark, we'll get the woodstove goin'."

"Why wait until dark?" the youngest Dawson boy asks. "It's cold enough in here now."

"Smoke," Scruff answers with a single bow of his head.

I'm sure I'm not the only one who gives him a blank look. Smoke . . . okay.

Then it's like a light bulb goes off. "Someone could see the smoke and know we're here?"

"Yup. After dark, they'll smell it but won't be able to see it. And if we keep the curtains closed and our lights low, that'll help too. Most of the time, I don't bother with a fire when I stop, but I can see how it'll help with the children and make them more comfor'ble."

"We'll get the horses put up," PJ says. "What'd you find for outbuildings?"

"The attached garage is probably our best bet," Donnie replies. "There aren't any cars in it. Should be enough room for the horses and the wagon."

"I hate keeping the horses on the concrete."

"Let's put 'em on highlines in the trees until it's time for bed, give them a chance to move around."

"Yeah, that'll be better, then we'll move them into the garage overnight."

The girls and I set up our beds in the living room, them in the tent and me in my sleeping bag alongside. Scruff takes the breasts off the geese he harvested, then slices and fries them alongside the rabbit the A Boy got. He also plucks the rest of the birds and puts the carcasses and legs in our two largest pots to stew overnight, adding to the bones from a rabbit we killed in Bakerville.

We brought a wooden box to store the soup pots with the lids on them, allowing us to simply add more water and reheat the frozen, congealed remains at each meal. Rochelle and I joke about the soup pot being like the nursery rhyme "Pease Porridge Hot." So far, our soup pot hasn't made it to nine days old, but that's only because we haven't been on the road that long.

Four goose breasts and a wild rabbit aren't enough for twenty-three people, so we make cornmeal mush, part of the supplies we brought from the mountain. I miss fresh food. We had several greenhouses on the mountain, which allowed us vegetables a few times a week. There were also cows and goats, giving the children milk each day.

I worry that, with our limited food, this trip might take a toll on Beth and Debbie. I don't want them to end up skinny and malnourished like Leanne's children. Of course, they walked around a thousand miles. Our entire trip, from the mountain lodge to my parents' home, is only a fraction of that.

While Scruff fusses over supper, the rest of us rummage through the house, looking for any usable items. From the little we find, it's obvious others have done this same thing. There's a bath towel crammed behind the headboard of the bed; it's dusty but otherwise fine. We also find several plus-size women's shirts and a roll of black thread with a needle nestled along the spool.

After our rummaging and dinner, the girls and I are sitting near our sleeping area. "Maybe Grandma will have hair dye," Beth says unexpectedly.

"Um, okay?" I answer. "Where'd this come from?"

"Oh, I was just looking at your hair. It's getting pretty gray."

I reach my hand to my right temple, where the hair is definitely coming in a lighter color than my usual dishwater blond. "Thanks for that, Beth. I really appreciate you pointing it out."

She shrugs. "Grandma did have several boxes of hair color in her bathroom closet, remember? We used to tease her about it. *You* even thought it was funny then."

"It was funny, especially since she had about fifteen different shades from blond to red. Some of those boxes were probably a decade old. But even if she still has them, I'm not sure I'd use it. I kind of like the natural look. It shows my wisdom, don't you think?" I waggle my eyebrows at her.

"Okay, Mom. Sure. Besides, Grandma probably traded them. I bet they'd be a hot commodity among women who still care about how they look instead of showing their wisdom." She gives me a smile to let me know she's teasing.

"Gee, thanks." Changing the subject, I ask, "How are you holding up? Do your feet feel okay in those boots?"

"Yeah, sure. They're pretty comfortable. I'm glad I'm on the snowboard instead of skis."

"I wish I could ski again," Debbie pouts. "It's boring sitting in the wagon all day. Sebastian tries to be funny and make silly jokes, but it's still boring."

"Maybe you can ski some tomorrow, at least long enough to stretch your legs," I say. "But for now, I think it's time you two crawled in your tent and went to sleep."

"Do you have your job tonight?" Debbie asks.

"Nope, not tonight. No sentry duty."

After the girls get in their tent, I move over to where Rochelle and Kimba are quietly talking.

As I scoot in next to them, leaning against the wall for support, Kimba says, "Some excitement today, huh?"

"Too much," I agree with a nod. "I mean, I know we talked about this happening, but I thought one of the big reasons we were leaving now was people wouldn't be out as much with the snow."

"That's the hope," Rochelle answers. "That and making sure we can all get where we're going before the worst of winter next year."

"How long do you really think it's going to take you to find Christopher and get back to Bakerville? Or, you, Kimba, getting the Dosens home?"

"Good question." Kimba motions with her hands. "Wish I knew. If everything went perfectly as expected, we'd have you home within the week. Rochelle would be reunited with her son a week after that. Less than three weeks later we drop off Leanne and her children in Lewistown. Then another two and a half weeks to get the Dosens and Dawsons where they're going. But . . . " She lifts her hands in a low surrender motion. "We've already discovered things don't go perfectly as planned."

"We knew the weather could still be an issue, but we prayed it'd be offset by safer traveling conditions," Rochelle says. "We suspect, once the snow subsides, it could be more dangerous. Unless the president's reconstruction efforts make it here."

"I can't imagine he'll give very high priority to such a rural area," I say. "Not with the way Wyoming and Montana are spread out and with such low populations."

"Right." Kimba nods. "But we must remember that a good part of the original destructions from the attacks and the nukes were in highly populated cities. I suspect any place that had a bomb is still high in fallout and won't be part of reconstruction yet."

"So they may be here sooner than we think?" I ask.

She shrugs. "Maybe? I long ago stopped trying to figure out government plans."

"And you used to work for them."

"Which is exactly why I don't pretend to understand."

"What exactly did you do for the government?" I ask.

She gives a slight shake of her head and then a wink. "If I tell ya . . ."

"Right, you'd have to kill me. I think I saw that movie."

"What movie?" Rochelle asks.

Kimba and I bust out laughing. I put my hand over my mouth to cover the noise.

"Shh," Kimba says. "We're going to wake the children, and none of us want that. I'm fairly sure Tamra was kidding."

"Yeah," I say, still giggling. "I was."

After a few more minutes of visiting, we all head to bed. While I don't have a watch shift tonight, Kimba is on final watch. She says she loves that one, mainly so she can watch the sunrise. Only she said it a lot more flowery, something like "a firsthand seat to God's glorious creation," or some such nonsense.

Chapter 12

"Tamra. Tamra."

I hear my name through a fog of sleep. I open my mouth and feel a hand lightly cover it.

"Shh. You need to get up. Stay low while you get your clothes on. Get the girls ready. You need to be ready to move."

The hand moves away from my mouth after I nod my agreement. By the light of the moon, I watch for a second as Rochelle moves on to the next sleeping figure before I crawl on my hands and knees to the girls' tent. I wake Beth and Debbie, keeping my voice soft while relaying the information to get dressed quickly.

"Is your rifle in the wagon?" Rochelle asks.

"My rifle and our ski gear." I nod, as I slip into regular snow boots. The girls and I, like most everyone else, had our outerwear inside to dry near the fire.

"Take the girls to the wagon. Load them up. Ready your rifle. PJ's already with the team. Do what he says."

"What's happening?"

"People are positioning to attack. Make sure you stay down." She crawls away.

With my heart pounding, I tell the girls to grab their packs, then we stay in a squat until we get to the windowless hallway. "Hurry to the open door at the end, that's the garage."

Once we reach the door, Leanne motions with her hands. "Squat down again and keep your head below the garage windows. Get the kids in the wagon."

In the dim natural light, I see PJ by the team, already connected to the wagon and waiting at the double garage door. Donnie's horse is saddled, secured by his lead rope.

I help Debbie and Beth into the wagon where Leanne's children and the two youngest Hoffmann kids are already scrunched in, sitting on their bottoms with their knees pulled to their chests.

"Where're your parents?" I ask.

"Dad was on outside watch when he saw the people coming," Nate Hoffmann says. "He called Atticus on the radio. Dad's still out there. Now Mom, Nicole, and most of the others are outside too."

"They'll draw them away." PJ's deep, calm voice provides welcome assurance. "Your dad will do what's needed, Nate. He'll let us get you all out of here. You, Robyn, and Leanne need to get in the wagon, too, with your guns ready. Rochelle will drive the team, and I'll take Donnie's horse."

The radio on PJ's belt makes a clicking noise. "That's the signal. We need to be ready to move."

"Where's Rochelle and Robyn?"

"Almost here," Leanne answers. "They're coming down the hall now."

"We ready?" Rochelle asks as she and Robyn spill into the garage.

"Is everything cleared out in the house?" PJ asks.

"I think so." Rochelle tosses a backpack on the floorboard of the wagon seat. "Someone left this behind." She sets a second, larger pack on top of the haybales lining the wagon. "Tuck it down inside, would you? And Robyn has the wet stuff we found in the house. We brought the stew pots that were on the stove out already. I'm going to take one more look through the house for anything else we need."

"I'll do that," Leanne says. "Fresh eyes are always smart."

"Good thinking," Rochelle agrees, while PJ instructs her to make it quick.

"Tamra, grab your rifle," Rochelle says. "You're on the seat next to me. Robyn and Leanne will get in the back. We'll be ready to go when we get the signal."

"We're just, what, busting out of here?" I ask.

"They'll engage them, try to draw them away," PJ says. "And if all goes well, we wait here until it's over. If things don't go well, we make a run for it."

"When will we know?"

"Anytime." PJ motions for Robyn to get in the wagon, then turns to Rochelle and me. "You two, keep your heads down. Stay on the floorboards until the last minute, Rochelle. Tamra, you can stay down and shoot from there. Keep your profile small. The wagon's overloaded, so everyone will need to hang on."

"What'll you do?" I ask.

"I'll open the garage door, make sure you all get away, then follow on the horse."

"Sounds like a terrible plan." I shake my head. Seriously terrible.

"No doubt," PJ answers as Leanne returns from the house.

"I didn't find anything." Leanne crawls into the wagon and perches herself on top of the haybales lining the edge. She does her best to scrunch her body down.

I'm crouched on the board next to the seat, with my backpack by my feet and my rifle in my hands. I touch the pistol on my hip, nervously checking if I can easily reach it. My hands are shaking so hard, I'm not sure I'll even be able to pull the gun and use it.

"We're going to be okay," Rochelle whispers.

"What's taking so long?" I ask. "It's been at least twenty minutes since you woke us up."

"I don't know. Maybe . . . maybe it's a false alarm?"

About a minute later, the radio makes another clicking noise and then there's a pause followed by a second click.

"They're getting ready to engage," PJ says. He still sounds calm. Assured.

So much for a false alarm.

"How will they let us know what we're supposed to do?" I ask.

"Radio— " His response is cut off by the sound of rapid gunfire. "Okay, be ready." PJ moves to the rollup door.

"God, we ask You to pull us under Your wings and provide Your protection." Rochelle pales as the gunshots continue. "Keep our group from harm. Step in and give us a miracle. We pray these things in Jesus' Holy Name, amen."

"Amen," PJ, Robyn, and most of the children echo.

"Ha," Leanne scoffs from her spot in the wagon. "God left us on our own long ago."

With several more shots, the sound of breaking glass fills the air.

"They're shooting at the house," Rochelle cries. "Do we need to go?"

"Not yet," PJ answers.

"Are the horses far enough away . . . you know, from the glass?" I ask, pointing to the high garage windows.

"They should be okay," PJ answers, some of the calm confidence fading from his voice.

"Great," I mutter.

It's many more minutes before the gunfire becomes sporadic instead of nearly constant. "Is less shooting good or bad?" I ask.

With her mouth in a harsh line, Rochelle gives a slow shake of her head. "I wish I knew."

After another minute or so, the shooting stops entirely.

"What's that smell?" Debbie asks from her spot in the wagon.

I take a deep breath but don't notice anything unusual.

"It might be from the gunfire," PJ says.

"Cordite?" I ask, nodding my head.

"Well, no. Cordite isn't used in modern ammunition, but many people still refer to the smell as cordite."

Then, a short while later, the radio cackles. "Hostiles down. We're coming in," Kimba says.

"Copy that," PJ responds, as Rochelle whispers, "Thank you, Jesus."

"Be patient," PJ says. "Let's just stay where we are until the group comes back."

"Is everyone okay?" Nate Hoffmann asks. "That was my mom, but what about— "

"We'll find out soon enough." PJ's words come out in a rush.

About a minute later, the radio sounds again. "There's smoke billowing from the house. Do you have a fire?"

I look to Rochelle, who gives me a wide-eyed shrug.

"Negative," PJ says.

"We're at the side door," Kimba says.

PJ unlocks the door. One of the twins is there holding up Donnie, who has one hand squeezing the other, wrapped tight with a blood-soaked bandanna.

"He was hit," the twin says. "Right through the center of his hand. Nasty looking."

Kimba steps in behind them. "I'll check out the situation in the house. Someone dig out the first aid kit. We'll need to work on that hand once we know the place isn't going to burn down around us."

"I doubt there's much you can do for it." Donnie's words have a slur to them.

"I'll start on Donnie," Rochelle says.

"Where's everyone else?" I ask.

"Making sure we didn't miss anyone," the twin says. "Don't want any surprises."

Kimba puts her palms on the door leading into the house. "Not hot. That's good. Tamra, you're with me."

Me?

I give a nod to hide my surprise. "Debbie, Beth, do whatever PJ needs."

Beth says something I don't quite catch as I hustle to Kimba's side.

"I don't think it's too much of a fire," she says. "But we need to get it out."

"Okay. How?"

"Here!" Robyn tosses me the damp towel we found and rinsed out earlier, then throws Kimba a shirt.

"Good." Kimba nods. "It's still wet too. Use one of the other shirts to keep pressure on Donnie's hand. We'll be right back."

Opening the door, a small puff of smoke wafts out. "Not too bad," Kimba says quietly. She turns on her pen light, keeping the beam low. A smoky haze fills the hallway. "There isn't too much smoke. Let's get it knocked out so we can take care of Donnie."

We check the door for heat before opening the bedroom on the right. It's fine and didn't even appear to have any smoke until we let it in.

Across the hallway is the room Scruff told us to stay out of. "This one?" I ask, hoping she'll say no.

"We best check it. You want me to do it alone?"

"You mind?"

With a slight shake of her head, Kimba moves to the door, pressing her hands against it to check for heat before reaching for the knob. "Should be fine." She opens it and steps inside.

I make a point of not looking in the room when the door is open.

She spends only a minute inside before returning to the hallway. "I checked the attached bath too. All clear."

After checking the final bedroom, we reach the end of the hall.

"Stay away from the windows. Rey's just finishing mopping up, and it should all be fine, but still . . . " Kimba moves the beam around the room. "Well, hello." She concentrates the light on the woodstove pipe where smoke's billowing from.

"They shot the stovepipe?"

"Looks like it." She moves the light to show glass on the carpet. We step to the stove. "See? Here's where it went in. Then straight on through and out the other side. We'd probably find the slug in the wall there. At least we don't have a fire to put out."

"Are we staying here the rest of the night?"

"I'm not sure. We'll have to see what Rey thinks when he gets back. For now, since we know the place isn't burning down, we're fine in the garage. Let's go take care of Donnie."

"Should we do something about the smoke?"

"Like what?"

"Maybe open another window and get a breeze while we wait for the fire to burn itself out?"

"Yeah, we could do that. Good thinking. Try to open the window without putting yourself in full view."

I open a small window over the kitchen sink while she opens the second window in the living room.

"Let's go take care of Donnie." She moves toward the garage.

"How will you know if Rey and the others are finished? You and PJ have the radios."

"They'll come back."

Back in the garage, Kimba asks, "How's it look?"

Donnie's on the concrete floor, lying on a sleeping bag with his hand propped up on a blanket. Leanne's on one side of him, and PJ and Rochelle are on his wounded side. Leanne makes a face and gives a slight shake of her head.

"I'm not sure what we can do for it." PJ's voice is guarded. "It's clear through."

"Is it still bleeding?"

"Seems to be slowing down a bit."

While Kimba kneels down next to Donnie, I notice Robyn and the Dosen twin are standing near the door, looking alert and cautious.

"Is something happening?" I ask.

"Not yet," the boy answers. "Did you get the fire out?"

"No fire." I proceed to tell him what we found.

"That's good. Right, Mom?" Debbie asks from the wagon. "Can we go back in and go to bed?"

"Not yet. We're going to stay out here. You can rest in the wagon while we wait for Rey and the others to return."

She makes a pouting noise and declares it's too small in the wagon with so many people.

"I can scoot over." Leanne's son moves as he speaks.

"And I'm getting out," Nate Hoffmann declares.

"That's fine," Kimba replies. "But I want Naomi to stay in the wagon and rest with Debbie."

"Mom?" Beth asks.

"Go ahead and step out. Stay at the back of the garage, out of the way."

While Kimba works on Donnie's hand, I remain near the door. After a few minutes, an owl hoots.

"That's my brother," the twin says, making his own owl noise in return.

"Really?" I ask in unison with Robyn.

"Yeah. I'm not sure if it's Atticus or Axel, but it's one of them." A few seconds later, another hoot sounds. "It's Atticus. Kimba, is it okay to open the door and let 'em in?"

"PJ, can you provide support?"

As soon as PJ's up with us, he tells me to stand along one wall and has Robyn near the door. He's next to Robyn and then tells the twin to open the door.

The other twin, both Dawson boys, and Victoria rush inside. Up to this moment, I didn't even miss Icky Vicky, but I suddenly wonder why she went out with the attack team when she doesn't even carry a gun.

"Where're the rest?" the brother asks.

"Rey and Nicole are following tracks," Atticus says. "They're trying to see where they came from to make sure we're not under additional threat. Scruff, Mom, and Axel should be here shortly. Donnie?" He motions with his hand to where Donnie's being treated.

"Go ahead. I've got the door."

"Thanks, little brother." He pops his twin on the shoulder.

Kimba and Rochelle have Donnie's hand cleaned and bandaged before Scruff and his group return.

"We're checkin' in and then gonna meet up with Rey and your daughter," Scruff tells Kimba. "It's gonna be daylight soon. What's your plan?"

"We need to see if they have a doctor in Belfry to treat Donnie," Kimba says.

"A doctor? What's the likelihood of that?"

"We had a medical team. It's possible they do too. How large is Belfry?"

I look to PJ; he lifts a shoulder. "Around two hundred, I guess. Does that sound about right, Tamra?"

"Somewhere in there. They used to have a volunteer fire department. No hospital. I doubt they even have a doctor's office, but maybe they had a vet."

"Ambulance service?"

I look to PJ, who gives a shrug. Adding my own shrug, I say, "I'm not sure about EMTs or paramedics. Truthfully, I'd be surprised."

"Well, we need to try, see if someone who has more skills can look him over."

Chapter 13

It's dawn before the entire gang is back together. Rey and his daughter Nicole followed the tracks backward. They found an empty camp suggesting it was just the six who attempted the attack. Scruff and his team, along with PJ and the twins, kept watch outside after checking in with us.

While the youngest children slept in the wagon, the rest of us took turns napping on the hard concrete or leaning against the wall of the garage. Staying together in the smoke-free garage made more sense than moving into the house.

Our limited medical kit contained disinfectant, gauze, and bandages, allowing Kimba to do a decent job wrapping Donnie's hand. I was surprised to discover we were supplied with a small number of painkillers, a scarcity in today's world. While most are over-the-counter mild analgesics, there's six narcotic tablets. Kimba gave him two of the OTCs and one of the heavy hitters in hopes of providing some relief from the gaping wound.

The goose and rabbit carcasses, which stewed for several hours before being moved to the wagon as we prepared our emergency getaway, are warmed up outside on a couple of the small camp stoves. Leanne takes it upon herself to feed Donnie. Watching her with him surprises me. As gruff as she usually is with him and the rest of us, she seems to be almost fretting over him.

Unfortunately, her kindness doesn't extend past Donnie. When I ask her how he's doing, she snaps, "How do you think?"

I lift a hand and, in my snottiest voice, say, "Excuse me for asking."

"There's no excuse for you," she mutters before scurrying away.

Yep. Loathsome Leanne. But not just loathsome, the way she switches from almost nice—never truly nice, but somewhat at least—to cruel in an instant is almost some kind of mental illness or something. I mean, really, who does that? Who's normal one second and downright nasty the next? Maybe I should call her Leanne the Lunatic.

"What's the plan?" Scruff asks as we put the food away. Although we ate most of the meat, we'll save the bones to boil out the marrow and as much nutrition as possible from our porridge pot.

"We're a little over halfway to Belfry," PJ says. "Yesterday, after seeing those folks at the state line, we made excellent time and are about three miles farther than we had planned. If we push hard, we can make it to Belfry before dark."

"We're operating on little sleep," Rochelle says. "I'm not sure how hard we can push."

"True." Kimba nods. "But we need to get someone with real medical knowledge to take a look at that hand."

"I'm fine," Donnie calls from his bed on the floor. "I'll probably never make a real fist again, but I'll manage."

"Are you right-handed," I ask, motioning to his bandaged left hand.

"Yep. At least that's the upside." His voice is heavy and thick.

"Still," Kimba says, "it'd be best for someone to look at it."

"Do you think the people we saw yesterday are the same ones who attacked us?" Rochelle asks.

Kimba and Rey share a look. "Hard telling." Kimba shakes her head.

"Occam's Razor," Rey adds.

"So, that's a yes?" Rochelle asks. "It's the simplest answer, so it's— "

"We don't know," Rey says. "None of us got a look at the people on the state line. But the camp we found was new. They hadn't been there long enough to pack the snow down much. There wasn't a firepit, nothing to indicate they'd done anything except set up. Thankfully, God was watching out for us. Him and the full moon, combined with the attackers' recklessness, kept us from being ambushed. It could've been a lot worse than it was."

"It's truly a miracle Donnie was the only one hit." Kimba steps closer to Rey. "And I think we should take a minute to thank God."

Within fifteen minutes of their little prayer session, we're on the road. Donnie's packed in the wagon with Leanne and the three youngest children. Our pace is slow but steady. We're barely covering a mile an hour, with the deep snow and the need to break trail combining with our exhaustion. It's not much slower than our usual pace, but it feels like a long, drawn-out slog.

PJ and Rochelle take turns driving the team, with one of them walking in snowshoes so someone else can ride in the wagon seat and rest. That works okay until the younger Dawson boy almost tumbles out when he falls asleep. We then decide to move the younger children onto the seat since they had the most sleep. With two of them sitting side by side, they keep each other occupied, too, allowing more space in the overloaded wagon.

At lunch, Leanne asks Donnie if she can use his snowshoes.

"Why don't you ride Gordie?" Donnie motions to his horse one of the A Boys is on.

"I'd rather walk for now. Maybe I'll ride later."

"You sure?" Kimba asks.

"Positive. I know those nurses didn't think I could walk." She makes a face, referring to the nurses on the mountain who believed Leanne and her children were in no condition to make this trip. "But today it seems I'm in no worse shape than most of you walking dead on your feet. Besides, it's too cramped in there with Donnie sprawled out and the extra bodies."

She lasts from when we get back on the road until our next break an hour later, then Kimba insists she goes back to riding. Even though she kept up with us pretty well, she was pale and her breathing sounded terrible. When we stop, she's even coughing and shaky. I hope she isn't coming down with something that spreads to the rest of us.

Less than an hour later, we reach a steep incline, a landmark I know indicates we're getting close to Belfry. Up this hill, down the other side, and then a long, flat stretch into town.

"Let's break here and get in a good rest before tackling that hill," Rey says.

"As steep as this one is—" PJ motions to the upcoming rise "—we may need everyone but Donnie out of the wagon. It might be too slick for the sleigh."

During the break, we come up with a plan to have only four people go up the hill: two people on skis walking side by side at a distance to mimic the sleds on the wagon, followed by two people on snowshoes. The thinking is, they'll break the trail for the wagon but won't compact it to the point of ice. Also, the snowshoe pattern the crampons leave might give the wagon a little more traction. Once the wagon reaches the top, the rest of us will follow.

I'm not convinced it'll work.

"Well, we might as well give it a try." Kimba lets out a loud breath, a misty cloud showing her exasperation. "You ready?" She motions to the oldest of the A Boys, who will walk alongside her, followed by Scruff and Rochelle in snowshoes.

They take their time trekking up the steep hill. Even with the skins on the skis, which provide a decent amount of grip, they struggle with slipping, whereas Scruff and Rochelle seem solid.

As soon as they reach the top, PJ makes a clicking sound with his mouth. "Here goes nothing. If this wagon starts sliding backward, you all better get clear." The horses take a couple of tentative steps. "Let's go, boys. We can do this." His mouth clicks again to get them moving.

I hold my breath, watching as they begin the climb.

Donnie's sitting up, staring back at us. He briefly argued he could ride his own horse since he was shot in the hand and not the foot, but the amount of blood he lost and his overall color suggest he might not even be able to sit in the saddle.

When they're halfway, one of the horses slip and the wagon slides to the side. The horse quickly regains his footing and digs in. Those of us watching let out a loud breath.

When PJ disappears over the top, Rey says, "That was enough excitement for one day. Let's get to the top and pray the people of Belfry welcome us with open arms."

While not exactly open arms, when we reach the roadblock set up well before the town of Belfry, the people manning it are at least cordial.

"Medical care?" one of the men asks after thoroughly quizzing us on whether our plans are to pass through or stick around. "We're low on supplies but might be able to get someone to take a look. We'll need to get approval. The only thing we're allowed to do is escort you through town."

He steps away from the barricade and moves to a beat-up old truck.

"Has himself a CB," Scruff whispers.

"A CB?" I repeat.

"Yeah, a Citizens Band radio."

"I know what it is, but how do you know he has one?"

"Antenna." He gestures with his chin.

I try to watch the man to see if he's talking on a radio, but I can't tell with the angle of the truck.

The man returns after a few minutes. "They'll take a look at your friend. You'll need to follow him." He points to a much younger guy. "They'll be expecting you at the hospital."

"Hospital?" I shake my head, sure that I remembered correctly before that this town didn't have any medical services.

"When did you get a hospital?" PJ asks.

"When the world fell apart," the man answers as he pulls up the collar of his heavy coat. "Best get a move on it. The wind's picking up, and it's going to be cold as soon as the sun drops."

The hospital is a restaurant along the highway I've had breakfast at several times before. Our group stops in the parking lot and is met by several men and a young woman in her twenties. "I'm Rhiannon Carpenter," she says. "I understand you have an injury?"

"Here," Donnie calls from his place in the wagon. "Got shot in the hand."

She makes a face and shakes her head. "Well, I'll take a look, see if there's anything we can do."

Rey and PJ help him out. After the narcotic earlier this morning, he refused the stronger stuff, saying we might need them later. He did take a couple of acetaminophen tablets, but that was at lunch. I can't imagine the pain he must be in.

Another man joins the woman leading Donnie into the former restaurant.

An older man, with weary gray eyes and sunburned cheeks showing above his salt and pepper beard, says, "My daughter and Lance will look him over, see if there's anything else that needs done. I suppose, since it's getting close to sundown and none too warm out here, we should find a place for you to stay. Does the old casino next door work for you?"

Before the collapse, Montana allowed slots and other forms of gambling. The old casino was a bar and restaurant with a small room housing a dozen or so slot machines. On the weekends, they'd have a live band.

Dallas and I went there on a date night once or twice when Beth was a baby, before Debbie was born. It'd been closed for several years before the attacks, having gone through many owners in the fifteen plus years I'd been driving this road regularly. It would sell and reopen for a short while, then shut down again. I seem to remember hearing it had recently sold and was going to be remodeled, but the attacks put an end to that—along with everything else.

"That'll be fine," Rey says in his fake voice. "We appreciate the hospitality and your daughter tending to our man."

"Was the gunshot accidental?"

"We were attacked."

"Nearby?" He stiffens.

"Almost a day's walk away. They aren't a threat to you."

"Took care of it, huh?"

"No choice in the matter."

"Yeah. That's the way it is now. We've been fortunate to have a break from hostilities over the winter. But we worry about what the spring will bring. Last summer, we escaped the worst of it. S'pose you all heard about the trouble Red Lodge had?"

Rey nods. "Bits and pieces. Some of our people needed medical care then, but the hospital was under siege."

"Yep. We got refugees from that fiasco. As far as we know, Red Lodge was a near ghost town before winter. I can't imagine the snow they got. They always get it worse than us, and we've been hammered this year. Nuclear winter is what some people are calling it. I heard you all are coming out of Prospector County. Did you escape the craziness in Prospect?"

"We were in Bakerville."

"Oh? What happened there? Some of our hunters went up to Robertson Draw for mule deer a few weeks back and said the plume of smoke looked ominous, like the whole town was on fire."

I glance at Robyn in time to see her eyes fill with tears. With more than a hint of sadness, PJ relays the information about the massacre and how there'd been a funeral pyre to take care of the remains. When the man asks who killed them, PJ dances around the answer.

"It was those jerks out of Prospect, wasn't it?" he asks, but instead of *jerks* he uses much more colorful language to describe them. So colorful, I motion for Beth to step away with Debbie while he goes off on his tangent. That, of course, earns me an eye roll from my oldest daughter.

After he finally calms down, which took some time as he shared what he's heard about the trouble being caused by not only Prospect but other towns around, he says, "You'll find a roadblock in Bridger too. That's the next town up the road."

"To be expected," Rey answers with a nod.

"Yeah, and I should warn ya," he says, rubbing his shaggy beard, "they started collecting a toll—cleared the road from Bridger to Fromberg and made it pay-to-travel."

"A toll?" Rey asks, instantly going on alert.

"Seen that in other places," Scruff says. "Summs a' thems nothing but robbers."

"It's not like that." Shaggy Beard shakes his head. "They're pretty fair, just doing what they need to do to keep their town alive."

"What kind of things are they looking for?" Rey asks.

"Food, supplies, anything useful. In this world . . . " He gives a shake of his head. "Every little thing matters. A guy that came through here last week said he gave them snow he melted and then boiled. Showed up at the check point—the one on the Fromberg side—without anything to trade, and they turned him away. Pretty smart to give them melted snow. There's plenty of white stuff around this year!"

"Why didn't he just go around?" I ask.

"I asked him the same thing. But since they're keeping the stretch clear, it seemed easier than going overland. Fromberg's the next little town past Bridger."

"Yeah, I know it," I say.

"So to his thinking, and I'd have to I agree with him, it's much easier to walk on cleared pavement than trudging through the snow. Seems the toll might be worth it."

"When you say cleared, what exactly do you mean?" PJ asks.

"Don't know. He made it sound like it's plowed or something. Easy walking is what he said. The stretch between the two towns is seven or eight miles. He said it was like an easy summer hike."

"Why'd they do that?" Rey asks.

Shaggy Beard shrugs. "To work together? Some of us talked about seeing if we can get in on their deal. It's only twelve miles between us and Bridger. Forming an alliance would be smart. Anyway, let's get out of this wind and get you settled for the night, then someone can go over and check on your man."

Chapter 14

Without a source of heat, the cavernous building is only slightly warmer than outside. We're setting up our tents on the hardwood floor when there's a loud bang on the door.

With sidearms at the ready, Rey, Kimba, and several others find defensive positions while ordering the children to the back of the building before PJ answers the knock.

"Not much they could do for me." Donnie steps inside followed by the woman and man from the makeshift hospital. "Said you all cleaned it up and now it just needs time to heal."

"And he'll need to keep it clean and dry," the woman says. "The main thing is to prevent infection. I'd like to change the bandage tomorrow before you leave. We're using fabric bandages now. I'll send a few strips with you so you can change it each day. Whoever will be helping with his wound care should join him at the hospital. I'll be there at seven o'clock. He said you have painkillers. Give him one to sleep tonight— "

"I don't need one." Donnie straightens, trying to look tough. A grimace crosses his face.

"Maybe not. But everyone in this building will sleep better if you take it."

I stifle a smile at her comment. Donnie has a gruffness about him when he's not injured. In the time since he's been shot, he's almost been docile compared to his usual brusqueness. Even though his people skills are often less than desirable, I think there's something more underneath the rough exterior.

I'm not the only one who thinks this. I overheard Jennifer talking with Rochelle about him during a break today, saying, "That Donnie puts up a tough exterior, but I'm beginning to think it's mostly an act."

"Why?" Rochelle asked.

"Why do I think that, or why is he acting?"

"Both."

"Why he does it, I don't know. Maybe he thinks that's the way he's supposed to behave. Do you know his brother Jerry?"

"I met him when they first showed up on the mountain, after we had the meeting about the atrocity that happened in Bakerville. You know PJ and the McCullough brothers knew each other before, right?"

"I'd forgotten that! I did hear about it but didn't really put it together. So PJ and Donnie are friends?"

"Not close friends. PJ knows his brother much better. They were members of the same church. Not Donnie, though. He'd show up to some of the men's events. According to PJ, his brother dragged him along kicking and screaming, but he'd enjoy it once he was there."

"Why doesn't that surprise me?" Jennifer asked with a small smile. "That explains a few things."

What it explained, I didn't find out. Debbie called out to me just then, and my eavesdropping came to an end. I'm sure it was some statement about how Donnie needs Jesus in his life in order to learn how to treat people properly. Jennifer's one of those all-out Jesus freaks who says things like, "Love always wins," and, "Treat others as you'd like to be treated." Or the one that always makes me shake my head, "We should be a beacon of love to the lost." *Okay, fine.*

While Jennifer is nice enough, I'm convinced she's faking it most of the time. No one can really be so loving and forgiving. Her inviting Icky Vicky Dawson and her boys to join them on their ranch still boggles my mind. I've concluded she must have only done it because they need the extra help. Two strong teen boys on a ranch would be an asset.

Of course, Victoria's youngest son isn't exactly what I'd consider a go-getter. The older one seems to be willing to help with anything needed, but the young one is on the lazy side—spoiled even, just like Vicky herself.

I doubt either of them ever did anything resembling work until the world fell apart. And since then, they've done the absolute bare minimum. They aren't exactly who I'd want helping me with day-to-day survival. Jennifer would've been much smarter to invite Kimba and her family to move to the ranch with them, though I doubt they'd agree. The Hoffmann family seems to have their heart set on helping rebuild our country.

I wish I could be more like Kimba—a true warrior. And even though I know she's also a Christian, she doesn't preach at me or anything like that. And I rarely feel she judges me like many of the churchgoers I've known.

Of course, I don't really get the judgment vibe from Jennifer either, but she's always so perfect—*and benevolent*—it's off-putting. Jennifer the Benevolent. It's really the perfect name for her.

~~~~~

I'm almost home! We stayed an extra day in Belfry so Donnie could regain some of his strength. As a thank you for the treatment he was given, a group of us helped the townspeople gather and split firewood along the river. They'd already harvested all the downed or dead trees in the small town's yards and within easy walking distance up and down the river.

In this area, trees are scarce unless there's a water source. We just don't get enough rainfall for them to grow as they do in more fertile areas.

The lack of trees might be odd for some, but I've always loved the wide-open spaces of Wyoming and Montana. Being able to see long distances—almost forever—is amazing. Living on the mountain over the winter, surrounded by trees, was almost claustrophobic at times.

Oh, there were advantages for sure. Firewood was one of them. With the surrounding forest, heating our homes wasn't something we worried about. And there's plenty for next winter and probably the winter after without having to venture far from the lodge.

Belfry has enough wood for the rest of this long, drawn-out winter, provided it ends somewhat when it should, but I have no idea how they'll provide heat next year. Their only hope is that the reconstruction efforts make it to Belfry before then, or they're going to be staying in frigid shells just like we did during our time there. With the temps hovering just below freezing and having a medium-strength wind, it wasn't terrible, but any colder and it could easily be deadly.

Donnie assured us he was well enough to leave yesterday, but I think it was mostly because none of us wanted to wear out our welcome. He's back on his horse, but obviously exhausted.

Yesterday, we didn't even make five miles before deciding to take refuge in one of the abandoned houses dotting the highway. At first, Donnie argued he could keep going after a short rest. But Rey
~~~~~

overruled him, insisting this was a good, defensible place to spend the night and we might as well take advantage of it.

Even though I didn't have watch last night, my sleep was restless. Every little sound would wake me up. I was sure we were being attacked again. Maybe tonight will be better.

After leaving the mountain about a week and a half ago, Joliet is now about three days' walk at our easy pace. The closer I get to home, the larger the knot in my stomach gets. What will I find there? Are my mom and dad okay?

As we've discussed many times, the world has gone crazy. Scruff and Leanne have each seen disturbing things while traveling. Neither of them talk freely about it. Leanne mostly just growls when the subject comes up, but Scruff has hinted about things he's seen. Their experiences may be similar, but the difference between the two is night and day.

While Leanne is bitter and convinced everyone's out to get her, Scruff is kind and helpful. He goes out of his way to be not only cordial to those of us he's now traveling with but also considerate.

Jennifer was spot on about him practicing the Golden Rule. Practicing isn't the right word—he lives it, just like Jennifer who goes out of her way to be annoyingly nice. It strikes me that, although I find Jennifer the Benevolent to be irritating, Scruff's kindness doesn't bother me. Why is that?

And I'm beginning to wonder if Leanne isn't putting up a front, just like Donnie and how he pretends to be crustier than he really is. Maybe Leanne's faking it too. Once in a while, I'll see a hint of something resembling a smile or Leanne'll talk in a voice that isn't full of anger or sarcasm. But then it's like she catches herself, realizing she's angry at the world and everyone in it and needs to show her hatred.

At least she's kind to the children, and not only her own two but the other young ones riding in the wagon as well. I was concerned her terrible demeanor would be a problem and she'd be mean to Debbie. I was surprised when we stopped yesterday afternoon to see Debbie laughing about a game of I-Spy the children were playing.

"Mommy, Leanne is the best at I-Spy," Debbie said. "She finds good stuff."

"Is that right?" I asked, glancing toward Leanne.

"It's fun. She makes the long ride go faster."

I shot a smile and nod of thanks to Leanne. She narrowed her eyes at me and spun on a heel. I don't know why I thought I'd get an agreeable response back from her.

I guess I should be happy she treats Debbie well. If she was cruel to her I'd . . . I'd . . . what would I do? Give her a major tongue-lashing that would accomplish little? I guess I'd just have Debbie walk with me. At least we're almost there. Our part of the journey will be over soon, and I won't have to deal with Leanne and her hot and cold personality much longer.

Tonight, we're camped only a few miles outside the town of Bridger, Montana, in a secluded bowl well off the highway. Like yesterday, we stopped early again today. Not only because Donnie is still struggling with his energy levels, but to ensure we approach the Bridger roadblock in full daylight—no reason to risk itchy fingers in the dark.

We discussed skimming the town and staying along the edge of the foothills, but with it being mostly private property, there's a risk with going that way too. So, for now, we're sticking with the state highway.

With the tents and the wagon set up in a circle, and our assortment of small camp stoves inside the circle—after warming our food, they're now providing a smidgen of heat—we finish up our evening meal well before the sun is ready to set.

The horses are in a nice copse of trees. Rochelle and PJ, with supervision from Donnie, moved snow so the three horses could get to the grass underneath to supplement their hay flakes and tree nibbles.

Instead of a tent, the wagon becomes Leanne and her children's cramped bed. A tarp is secured over the top, making it, according to Leanne's son, a warm and cozy fort. I wonder if he'll find the too-small backpackers tent we're using, which will soon be passed to his family, fort like. My guess is he'll love it. His mom, not so much.

"Just like last night, we'll go with two on each sentry shift," Rey says. "Even though it's clear, you'll have less moon than last night, so keep your ears open."

Debbie lets out a laugh. "It's funny when you say that. My ears are always open."

"Well, tonight, Miss Debbie, you can keep your ears closed so you can get some sleep."

"What about my mom?" she asks, pointing to me.

"Your mom gets to be the first one up in the morning."

"Oh, goody." I clap my hands in fake enthusiasm, which garners a laugh from Debbie and the usual eye roll from Beth. No surprise there. Although I want to take my turn at watch, I'm nervous about it. I had a shift in the Belfry building, but that felt different. *Safer.*

Camped here, near the town, feels exposed. Even though we're well hidden from the road, we'd be easy to find—easy to attack. I just hope I can be alert and aware enough, like Rey was, to prevent anyone from sneaking up on us.

"I knew you'd be excited." Rey smiles. "Kimba, you'll be excited right along with her. You two are on last shift together." Rey goes on to assign the rest of the watch schedule. When he's done and has just finished saying we should wrap it up for the night, a long, deep howl sounds in the distance.

"The coyote sounds sad," Debbie says.

I purse my lips as I listen to his mournful cry. I shake my head. "I don't think it's a coyote."

"A wolf?" Scruff asks.

"Yup," PJ answers. "There's a known pack in this area."

"That's right," Donnie says. "A guy killed a huge black one a couple years back. I saw a picture of him holding it up like a fish, and it was as tall as he was. But they aren't just in Joliet. They're everywhere, have been for years. I'm surprised we haven't heard any before now."

"We might be hearing the sanctuary," I say, as the wolf song continues.

"Sanctuary?" Donnie asks. "Whatcha mean?"

"There's a wolf sanctuary west of Bridger."

A chorus of voices respond in surprise.

"Never heard of that," Donnie says.

I shrug. "It's a fascinating story. They're buffalo wolves thought to have gone extinct in the early 1920s. But McCleery, a doctor from Pennsylvania, began buying wolf pups in hopes of preventing their complete extermination. He got quite a pack and was breeding them. After he died, someone else took them over, moved them to a new location, and so on and so on until they eventually ended up here."

"Buffalo wolves?" PJ asks. "Are they a subspecies of the gray wolf?"

"Maybe? I think they're also called the Great Plains wolf."

"Now that you're talking about it," Rochelle says, "I remember learning about them in school. And yes, they are a subspecies of the gray wolf. In North America, there's only the gray and red wolf. The red has only a few hundred and is on the endangered species list. And, if I remember correctly, the Plains wolf was the most common of the grays at one time."

"Yeah, well, you know what I think?" Donnie leans forward to make his point. "Wolves are big-game killers. Reintroducing them to Yellowstone was stupid."

"Agreed," Scruff says. "I don't like the idea of anything dyin' out, but I've heard tell of nothin' but trouble with them wolves comin' back. Why, they didn't even give all y'all the right kind of wolves."

"That's right!" Donnie exclaims, his voice loud and confident. "They aren't even the same kind that used to live in Yellowstone!"

"They did help the ecosystem," I offer weakly.

"Ha! By killing the elk!" Donnie says.

I give a slight shrug. He's not wrong. When this was a hot topic between Dallas and Jackson, I wanted to understand their concerns and did some research. Turns out, before the wolves were reintroduced in the '90s, there were many trees and plants the elk were eating down to nothing.

After the wolves, the trees and grasses have improved. There's a big, long explanation for it, but part of it is the elk and deer are being eaten by the wolves and the predators also change the habits of the prey. So . . . yeah. The wolves do kill the elk, but they also help the ecosystem.

"How would a wolf sanctuary even be operating right now?" Beth asks. "Don't places like that need donations? Remember when we went to that wildlife sanctuary, Mom? They charged us a fee to get in, saying it helped feed the animals. And then you got on their mailing list, and they were always asking for money."

"Good point." Donnie nods. "They probably turned them all loose. Those beasts are running wild and wreaking havoc. What'll happen if they're breeding with the wild wolves?"

"Nothing will happen," Leanne snaps. "It's not like you're going to get zombie wolves." She mutters *idiot* under her breath.

Several voices talk at once, discussing whether the sanctuary would just turn them loose or what they would do.

"Hold on, folks." Donnie lifts his uninjured hand. "While I don't care much for the mangy things, some of the stuff I'm hearing isn't quite on track. Beth, you girls— " he motions to the three teenage girls, their heads pressed together, looking pale " —I don't think you need to be concerned about the wolves bothering us. The elk and deer, they'll wipe them out for sure, and that's no doubt a problem since we're relying on them for our food. But they won't bother us none."

"Well . . . " Scruff strokes his wild beard. "There's been reports of wolves killin' humans."

I shoot him a look.

Scruff lifts his hands. "They're not common, y'all are right about that."

"Donnie's right," PJ says. "But so is Scruff. In historic times, wolves may have attacked humans, but it just doesn't happen anymore."

"Um . . . hello." Scruff gestures around. "Y'all think that's not what's happened here? Been thrust back a hundred—make that two hundred years. The world's gone boom, an' here we are. Long ago, wolves were killed off as man took over their land. But now, the tables . . . look how they've turned. It's man who's getting killed off. Natural predators are gonna be the ones taking over. Some of them predators are on two feet, no doubt. But there's gonna be four-footed ones too."

Scruff's proclamation opens up a whole new conversation about what we can expect from predators in this new world.

After a couple minutes of intense debate, Rochelle says, "Tamra, do you know how many they had at the sanctuary?"

"How many wolves? Fifty? Sixty? I'm not sure. It's been a while since I've heard anything about them."

"Was it a breeding facility?"

"Maybe? I don't really remember."

"Okay, well, that was an exciting story," Rey says. "But it's time to sack out. And as you're on watch, remember, a wolf howl can be heard for miles. The one singing to us is probably at least four or five miles away."

Right around where the sanctuary is.

The wolf songs continue with not just the one but others answering. Surprisingly, neither Debbie nor Beth are overly bothered by them. When living on the mountain, we expected to see and hear wolves, but we never did. Around Thanksgiving, a pack was near the ski lodge. Debbie spent many days with her nose pressed to a window, searching for one.

Before Debbie falls asleep in our tiny, thin-walled tent, she asks, "Do you think I'll finally get to see a wolf?"

I don't have the heart to tell her that I certainly hope not. It's one thing to see a wolf when safe inside the ski lodge or our cabin. It's entirely something else when we're hotfooting it across the state and sleeping in tents—something else entirely.

Chapter 15

Well before Scruff or PJ, who have the guard shift before mine, come knocking on the tent to wake me, I slowly begin to dress, doing my best not to disturb the girls in this tiny tent.

The last of my sleep was restless and interrupted—not with worry of wolves outside my tent, but with dreams of my dead husband Jackson. Nightmares, really. As I slip on insulated pants, the scenes from the dream replay in my head. I give my shoulders a shake, trying to rid myself of the visions.

I thought I'd be happy with Jackson, thought he was so much like his brother that we'd make a good team.

I was wrong. Terribly wrong.

My shift starts at three o'clock and lasts until six, though I suspect it'll end slightly earlier. Usually, once the sun starts doing its wake-up dance, people start filing out of their tents. Many of our internal alarms are set by the daylight. Living these many months by the rise and set of the sun has really changed our biorhythms.

Dallas would've fit in perfectly with our new early rise lifestyle. He was always a morning person. There were so many times I'd stumble out of bed and he'd already been up for hours. When will the ache of missing him ever subside?

As I step into the heart of our camp, I long for the small flame from one of our camp stoves and a cup of hot coffee warming over it. We have an assortment of lightweight stoves, some of which work better than others, with the rocket stove design ones burning the best—at least that's what PJ calls them. Two of them are from his personal supplies from his time as a professional hunting outfitter. The others—one provided for each family except mine—aren't quite the quality but still warm our food.

We were given generous rations when we left our mountain home, but coffee wasn't one of those. I wonder how long it'll be before coffee, chocolate, bananas, and other things that don't grow locally are part of our diet again. Coffee and chocolate can still be found, packaged and turning stale, but bananas are certainly a thing of the past. And oranges—I'd love an orange.

At least we have the wild game. I suspect places like Florida, where they can grow oranges and other citrus, are wishing they could kill a big elk. Of course, since leaving the mountain, we haven't seen signs of elk.

PJ said it was surprising we had as many as we did over the winter. Resident herds will sometimes stay at the higher elevations, but most migrate to the basin, browsing fallow fields and waiting out the winter.

This winter we had enough elk for our small community to not only survive, but when combined with the livestock brought up the mountain, we essentially thrived. Our diet may have been boring with the focus of meat, field corn, barley, and sugar beets, but we're essentially healthy.

We expected to see elk once we reached the basin, but so far it's just been deer, mainly whitetail instead of muleys, and the occasional antelope. Could it be the wolves have been causing such a ruckus the elk are steering clear? And will we see less deer and antelope now that we're near the wolf sanctuary?

I hope the wolves haven't killed too many of the deer and that Joliet has enough game to support the town and add three more to its fold.

"G'mornin', Tamra," Scruff says in his slow, welcoming way.

"Good morning. I can take over if you want to head in."

"'Bout time enways. Your partna' oughta be out shortly."

Just then, Kimba's tiny tent begins to shake. After a momentary struggle with the zipper, she frees herself. As she steps out, I shake my head. Even at this insanely early hour, walking across the backcountry in the middle of winter, she looks good.

Too good.

Her blond hair and Barbie doll like beauty refuse to be contained, no matter her circumstances. Next to her, I feel completely homely. My lackluster dishwater hair is lank and dirty. I have it in a braided bun, but it doesn't help the fact it's disgusting.

I should've washed it the night before last when we were in the house with the woodstove warm enough to keep my hair from freezing before it could dry. The girls and I both took quick sponge baths, but hair washing was just too much effort.

If I'm not more diligent with my hygiene, I may soon be on par with Icky Vicky and her lack of cleanliness; although, she does seem a little more put together now than she was on the mountain.

Those couple of days we waited out the storm in Bakerville at the beginning of our journey, she even took a wide-tooth comb to her hair and removed the snarls. She also smells better than she did, but she's not nearly as put together as Kimba. None of us are.

How does Kimba do it? How does she manage to look fresh from the spa when she's been living in the same conditions as the rest of us?

"See?" Scruff juts his chin in Kimba's direction. "I'll let ya two visit for a couple of minutes while you wake up. Atticus and me'll take another walk around. Quiet night af'n those wolves stop'd their racket."

I subconsciously tuck my lackluster locks under my stocking cap and give Kimba a smile.

"Hey, Tamra." She gives a shiver. "That thin tent was holding in more heat than I thought."

"Yeah. They're definitely better than nothing."

"We're very blessed our friends were so generous with outfitting us for this trip."

"It's for sure better than nothing."

"Oh, I know not everyone was happy about it, but they really were amazing. You know the saying, 'You might be the only Bible some people read'?"

"No . . . I don't think so."

"Oh. It's something the chaplain was talking about." She leans closer to me and, in a quiet voice, says, "I'll admit, I'd never heard it before he said it either."

I give her a smile.

"He was talking about how people in the church—you know, those of us who consider ourselves Christians—should make a difference to others, not just to our family but also to our community. As Christians, we ought to live in a way anyone watching will know we're spoken for."

"Spoken for . . . " I repeat, not understanding.

"You know, by God."

"Oh, sure. Right."

"Like how Jennifer makes a point of treating people well."

"Her Golden Rule thing." I nod. "Though, I'll admit, I think she takes it to the extreme."

"Does she?"

"You don't think so? I mean, look how Leanne is. Jennifer still goes out of her way to give her a smile when all she gets in return is a scowl. She makes sure Leanne and her children get large portions of food. The things she does . . . " I shake my head.

"Jennifer definitely lets her light shine. We all should. We need to portray Jesus Christ to those around us who are hurting and struggling." She gives a shrug. "Because some people might never pick up a Bible, but they can see us, see how we're living like Jesus . . . or not. Leanne's having a rough time right now. We need to show her that good still exists, not just the evil she's encountered."

"And you're a Christian and want to show that?" I ask.

"*Now* that I'm a Christian, I want to show it." She gives me a combination nod and shrug accompanied by a smile. "I thought I was a Christian before, but I didn't know the truth then. Rey and I used to go to this big, really fun church near our house. Not all the time." She lets out a small giggle. "Not even too often really. But we'd go when they'd have some kind of big event. I thought—*I was sure*—I was a Christian. It wasn't until the chaplain on the mountain was talking about how going to church didn't make you a Christian any more than standing in the middle of the garage makes you a car—another of his sayings—I started wondering what I was missing."

"What were you missing?"

"The Gospel."

"The Gospel." I repeat with a nod, as I pretend like I'm following what she's telling me.

"I'll tell you— " She shakes her head. "When I finally understood my sin . . . I mean, the *wages* of my sin would mean my death for eternity and separation from God, I knew that wasn't what I wanted. I wanted more. I wanted to be surrounded by His glory.

"One of the songs we used to sing at the super church we attended—did I tell you they had a rock band? That was pretty cool. I just wish they would've told me about the truth then. Anyway, the song was about imagining what heaven is going to be like, wondering if we'll dance for Jesus or fall at his feet or sing or be speechless. Now I know, when I'm surrounded by His glory, it's going to be perfect. And even better, my husband and children know this too. Learning about God and His son, Jesus, has changed our lives. And I most definitely want to be the Bible for people. I want my love for Jesus reflected through my life."

I stare at her with wide eyes. Kimba the Spy and Secret Agent Rey are not what I thought. With all the Bible reading and praying, I figured they were churchy people, but not to the extent she's implying now. I guess I thought maybe they were just going along with it because it was kind of expected.

Jennifer and her sons are what Dallas and I would've referred to as Holy Rollers. Rochelle and PJ, too, but to a lesser extent. Kimba and her family seemed more subdued.

And the stories I'd heard about Rey and Kimba—big, scary stories about the terrible things they'd done—they're probably more fiction than fact, but it's no secret she's killed people. In recent months, she'd been forced to take lives when we were attacked by people both outside and inside our community.

And here she is, going on about imagining what heaven will be like. And the look on her face as she talks . . . she's like a kid at Christmas. Only for her, God and His son are her greatest gift.

"I, uh, appreciate your feelings on this, but . . . " I shake my head. "I'm not sure it's for me."

"Why's that?"

I let out a slow breath. "While I don't deny there may be a God, I'm certain He's not interested in me. If He was—well, look at this mess we're in."

She gives me a smile. "I think there's lots of people asking this same question. Why would a loving God allow this? But He's not just loving. He's holy, holy, holy. That means— "

"Please, Kimba." I raise my hand. "I appreciate your . . . your enthusiasm for this, but . . . " I shake my head. "It's probably time for us to relieve Scruff and Atticus."

"Sure, it probably is." She offers me a smile. "Let's find out what they've been doing on their watch and then we'll do something completely different." She notches up the smile and adds a wink.

As we turn to walk away, she stops and puts her hand on my shoulder. "You might not want to hear about it, but He's here for you too. God's here for you if you just ask Him. You got a raw deal. Most of us know that. Don't think for a minute the sins of your husband are also your sins."

"I can't— " I choke on my words. "I should've known."

"Really? There's plenty of stories about spouses married much longer than a few months who had no idea what their partner was doing. Your husband was a serial killer."

The sting of her words hits me like a smack across the face.

"Yeah, I know. It sounds harsh, and it is. But we found enough evidence to show he killed at least three women we personally knew in the community, right?"

I drop my head as my tears fall. The day Jackson died in a freak accident, an avalanche while they were out looking for a missing girl, my heart shattered—two husbands both lost to me.

Dallas and I loved each other deeply and passionately, a love producing two amazing children. Jackson was there when I needed him, grieving along with me over the loss of Dallas. My love for him came as a surprise, and while it didn't have the passion, it was comfortable and necessary. *Like an old shoe.* The kind that was well-worn and safe—no way could I ever stumble or fall while wearing that well-worn shoe. But it was still love.

And he treated the girls wonderfully. As their uncle, he already loved them. I knew he had strong opinions about things and could get passionate when sharing his beliefs, but he never raised his voice or his hand toward any of us.

When he died, I was lost and alone again, grieving like a widow should. But a few weeks later, as I was cleaning out his things to take usable items to the community supply house, I was gutted.

Finding an old cigar box full of jewelry was surprising. A toe ring with a small ruby in it was the first piece I picked up. Putting down the toe ring, I pulled out a necklace with a hummingbird pendant, then a second with a diamond cross. There was a plain, thick silver chain too. When I pulled out a charm bracelet, my heart stopped.

I recognized the bracelet.

I'd noticed one of the charms in the breakfast line: a silver cow. The bracelet owner, Phoebe Baker, one of the young women living on the mountain, told me with great animation how her dad thought it'd be amazing to give her a cow charm since he owned a cattle ranch.

She then went on to point out her favorite charm: a globe. She said she loved the globe because, whenever she looked at it, it reminded her of how she was going to travel the world as soon as she was old enough. "Of course," she said, "I have to wait until the planes start flying again, but it'll happen. I'm still young, and I'll have plenty of time." It was only a few days after our conversation she was found dead.

Murdered.

My fingers moved slowly from the cow to the globe, carefully caressing the cat and heart charms between the two.

I debated for over an hour on what to do. I could've kept it quiet, preserved the reputation of my dead husband who'd be unable to defend himself from accusations.

And there would be accusations, of that I had no doubt.

When I took the box to the mountain police, my life changed again. The hummingbird necklace belonged to the girl they were looking for—and later found dead—when the avalanche killed Jackson. The toe ring belonged to another woman who died under suspicious circumstances before everyone moved up the mountain.

The rest of the jewelry, half a dozen pieces, belonged to unknown people. It's generally accepted he killed six more women and kept trophies of their murders—a typical serial killer trait.

I meet Kimba's eyes. Instead of condemnation, there's kindness. And maybe even understanding.

Chapter 16

A small band of light is on the horizon when Donnie makes his way from his one-man tent to the sitting area. "Mind helping me light one of the stoves?" he asks when he sees me. "I think I'll have some of that awful mint tea."

After getting the fire going and putting on a small pot of water to heat, I ask him how he's feeling.

"Like I have a hole in my hand," he says.

"Yeah." I give a slight nod as I move away from him.

"Sorry," he mutters. "The stupid thing throbs. And now my stomach's upset. Thought the tea might at least help with that."

"Let me get the tea out for you. Do you have your bag? And a cup?"

He lets out a sigh. "The dumb fabric teabag is in one of my saddle bags. The cup's in my pocket." He pulls a short and squat insulated cup out of the pocket of his jacket.

"Do you want to use my teabag?"

"If you don't mind. I'd appreciate not having to dig for the thing."

I give a nod. "You mind keeping an eye out for me? I'm still on watch."

"Where's Kimba?"

"She took the high ground." I motion toward a small crag.

"She climbed that thing in the dark?"

"Nah, just went up to the edge of it, said it'll give her an advantage."

"Makes sense. Thanks for loaning me your teabag."

The cloth teabag, part of the rations given on the mountain to each of us, is in the outer pocket of my backpack, which is folded in a plastic tarp by my tent. None of us have tents large enough to keep our packs in. It was PJ's idea to bring thick pieces of plastic to make little cocoons for each of the packs.

Because of our shorter distance and the convenience of the wagon, Beth, Debbie, and I have smaller backpacks than most of the others. Even though my bag is smaller, by the end of the day it still feels like a lead weight on my back. I considered wearing it when doing my nighttime patrols but instead opted for filling my pockets with essentials I might need. I don't want to carry the thing a minute more than necessary.

I take a minute to fill the teabag with my personal supply of tea leaves before straightening and stretching my back and then heading back toward Donnie and the fire. As I twist, the wagon moves slightly, then the tarp lifts and Leanne stumbles out.

"Good morning," I say quietly, attempting the kindness thing that seems to work so well for Jennifer.

Leanne begins to lift her hand but seems to reconsider before giving me a solemn nod. At least it wasn't a scowl.

"Here you go." I offer the bag to Donnie.

"Hey, thanks for filling it too."

"It wouldn't do you much good empty." I shoot him a smile.

Leanne, now sitting at his side, says, "Aren't you supposed to be on watch?"

I give her a fake salute before turning to go back on my roving patrol.

"C'mon, Leanne, don't be like that. Tamra was doing me a favor, and I was keeping an eye out for her."

"You're in no condition to be doing her job."

I'm partway across the camp, but in the quiet of the early morning, Donnie's voice carries clearly. "I don't know why you don't like her."

I step behind the nearest tent, allowing it to obscure me from their view. I'd like to know why she doesn't like me too.

Where Donnie's deep voice was easy to hear, I strain as Leanne gives her response. "Like her? I don't care about her one way or another. I just don't see why she can't make that last little bit of the journey on her own."

I narrow my eyes. She's still stuck on that? What's it with her thinking my girls and I should make the trip from Fromberg to Joliet without the rest of the group? It might only be ten miles, but who in their right mind would travel that in today's world without the protection of others?

"Really?" Donnie asks. "She's a woman alone with two kids."

"So? I've been alone plenty of times since this disaster happened. I kept my kids safe all by myself. You think she's not as capable as me? I thought Wyoming girls were supposed to be tough?"

"You were alone, alone? I thought you were with— "

"Not always. We were separated a few times. We were fine. She'd be fine, too, if she wasn't such a baby."

"Look at my hand, Leanne. A few days ago, we were in a shootout. Attacked. We assume it was just for the few goods we have, for our horses. You really think Tamra and her children should be out here alone?"

Leanne responds but her voice is too low for me to hear.

After a few moments, Donnie says, "I just think you should ease up on her. It's not like you're going to convince Rey or the others to let her finish the trip on her own. You might as well stop going out of your way to treat her so poorly."

"Oh, puh-leeze. Treat her poorly?" This time her voice has a slight whine to it. "Like I said, she doesn't matter. Let's get her where she's going—going an extra twenty miles out of our way to do so—and then I never have to see her again. Who cares? Now enough of that. How's your hand feeling?"

As they change the subject to his injury, with a shake of my head, I continue my route. What a ridiculous woman. Twenty miles out of their way? It's only a few extra days on the road. It's not like it should matter that much to her since she usually rides in the wagon anyway.

Walking around camp, attempting to focus on my patrol, I keep replaying her words in my head. I should've said something, should've stepped out and made myself known and made sure she knew that I heard everything she said. I don't matter to her? Fine. She doesn't matter to me either. But she'd better stop being such a snot or . . . or she'll be sorry.

Looping back around, the sun is rising enough Donnie and Leanne are now easily in view from the far end of the camp. And what a view it is.

I catch them in a lip lock! I put a hand over my mouth to stifle a giggle. For all of Leanne's posturing, dirty looks, and attitude directed at Donnie, here she is making out with him. I don't even know what to think about it. I mean, she's a single adult—widowed when Sebastian was a baby—and Donnie's never been married . . . but still. Maybe him getting shot made her realize feelings she didn't know she had.

In some ways, they're a good match. Both have abrasive personalities, and both tend to want to always get their way. Well, maybe not Donnie as much as Leanne. Of course, it's probably nothing more than a fling. Leanne has told Donnie many times that he won't be welcome at her aunt's home in Lewistown. Donnie's responded that he knows, that he just wants to make sure she and the children get there safely and then he'll head back to Bakerville.

They finally pull back, staring each other in the face. Donnie reaches up and caresses her cheek with his good hand. I'm too far away to hear his words, but I can see his lips moving as he speaks. His overgrown mustache makes it difficult to do any lip reading, not that lip reading is a skill I possess, but I swear he says, "We should get married."

This thought is confirmed when Leanne throws back her head and laughs, which stops abruptly as she covers her mouth, realizing it's barely dawn and people are sleeping.

I take several steps, moving within hearing distance. I should let them know I'm here. It's one thing to eavesdrop when I'm the topic of conversation, but this is private, personal.

I softly clear my throat—maybe a little too softly.

"You don't want to marry me," Leanne answers. "I'm . . . I'm a mess. You know that."

"We're all a mess right now. Besides, I understand your struggles. I can help."

"Maybe you should've brought this up before, when we were still living on that mountain."

"Yeah, maybe. But getting shot made me realize I only have a limited number of days until God calls me home."

My eyes go wide. Is Donnie another one of *them*? A Bible thumper? With the way he acts, I wouldn't think so. If Kimba's little saying about being the only Bible people read were applied to Donnie . . . nope. No way.

"You know how I feel about God these days," Leanne says. "Bringing Him into this isn't the way to sway me."

"Maybe not. I'm not religious, you know that. But what if God is waiting— "

"Enough, Donnie. I thought you were just as disillusioned with God as I am."

"Disillusioned?" He shakes his head. "I've just never made time for Him. My brother, he was a churchgoer, met PJ and his family there. Me, though—nope. But I'm beginning to wonder if I'm the one who didn't have my priorities straight. Some of the things happening . . . "

He lifts his hands. "The things you've told me about your life, it doesn't make sense— "

A tent zipper rattles, causing Leanne and Donnie to look in the direction of the noise.

Seeing me standing there, Leanne smirks. "Spying on us?"

Trying to keep a guilty look off my face, I lift a hand. "Just making my rounds."

"Yeah, right."

I give Leanne my sweetest, fakest smile before turning to bid good morning to Rey. The camp quickly comes alive as more tents shake and more zippers rattle.

Leanne motions to me, beckoning with her finger, just as Rey asks, "Quiet night?"

"Perfectly." I turn away from Leanne to give Rey my full attention. "Kimba?"

After telling him where she went, he says, "I suppose I'll start getting the children up so we can break down camp. That's a chore that loses its luster fairly quickly."

"Pretty much all of this— " I motion my hands in a circle " —has lost its luster for me."

"Lord willing, a few days and you'll be home."

"Um, yeah. But you guys, you have no plans to go home to . . . " I shake my head as I try and remember the city they're from.

"Denver? Someday, sure. With the population there and the way things could get before the rest of the country fell apart, we're not sure what we'd find. Our condo was right next to one of the bridges that was destroyed in the early attacks. That's why we fled, how we eventually ended up in Bakerville. But once we get everyone else in our little traveling troupe settled and join up with whoever's running the rebuilding, if they felt we'd be the most useful in Denver, that's where we'd go."

"Don't you worry about the children? Your children, I mean, with hauling them all over the place with the way things are? Taking your daughter with you when you went after those . . . those . . . "

"The ones who shot Donnie? Yeah, sure. We know it's a risk. Nicole's seventeen. She's been training with the militia since we moved to Bakerville. She knows what she's doing, but it doesn't change my concern for her. Sure, I'd like to surround her in bubble wrap and lock her in a room. What parent wouldn't? But we can't live our life like that."

"There's a big difference between locking them in a room and purposely taking them out into the dangers of a broken world."

"True. But you're doing the same thing. I assume you weighed the pros and cons of staying on the mountain or going to your parents' house."

"Sure, but— "

"And Rochelle. She knew she had to go after her son but decided the risk was too great to take her daughters. Kimba and I spent a lot of time in prayer and reading the Word. We're new at trusting in God, but we both feel—*we believe*—we were told to go, to fulfill our obligation to Jennifer and her boys, and to our country. Something's gone terribly wrong, and if we can help make it right, we want to do so."

"How?"

"Don't know. But it's certainly interesting the things the president says. And what he doesn't say. Or how we don't hear from anyone but him. It makes my spidey senses go on full alert."

"What do you mean?"

"Tamra, may I speak to you?" Leanne asks in a clipped tone.

"Good morning, Leanne." Rey smiles. "I was just going to get my children up."

"Good morning." She gives him a nod as he turns away. She takes me by the elbow. "Over there."

I shake my arm. "Seriously?"

"Just— " She takes a deep breath. "Please may I speak with you privately?"

I start to tell her no, but an image of Jennifer with her smiling face, always going out of her way to be nice, fills my head. "Okay, fine." I motion her to follow me to the edge of the camp.

Once we're there, with her voice low, she says, "I'd appreciate if anything you thought you saw or heard was kept quiet."

"*Thought* I saw?" I raise my eyebrows.

Her cheeks flush. She lets out a loud breath. "Please? I don't . . . I want to talk to my children before they hear any camp rumors."

"I'm not a gossip."

She furrows her brow. "No, I suppose you're not. I know you probably understand what it's like."

"What it's like?"

"To be the topic of conversation. But the way I hear it, tongues were wagging over things you didn't do. At least the rumors that went around about me were mostly true. I'm a mean, nasty heathen." Her expression is a cross between serious and teasing.

"Why is that?"

She shrugs. "What do you care?"

I snort. "I don't *care*. But it sure seems you go out of your way to be . . . disagreeable."

She screws up her mouth and gives me a hard look. "What? You think I should be friendly? Become best buds with you and the others here? In a few days, you'll be in Joliet, after we go out of our way to get you there."

I start to argue, but she raises a hand. "I know, I know. It's the *right* thing to do. I've heard it over and over. We'll leave you there and go on. Will I ever see you again? Nope. So why should we be friends?"

"I don't care if we're friends, but how about not going out of your way to be such a . . . such a— " I shake my head. "Look, whatever you and Donnie have going on, I'm not going to say anything. Truthfully, I'm happy for you. While he's a bit much sometimes, it seems he's genuinely fond of you, even when you're unpleasant to him."

She gives a nod as a slight smile crosses her face. "He is persistent. And while he can be rather blunt, he's—never mind. It's not really something I need to explain to you."

I snort again. "Right. Fine. As you said, we're not friends, so why pretend we are?" I spin on my heel and leave her standing there.

Chapter 17

Once we start moving, it takes only a little over an hour to reach the roadblock in Bridger, situated less than a half mile from the junction of Montana Highway 72 and US Route 310, the road that runs down the middle of the small town and doubles as Main Street. Breathing in the crisp morning air, I glance around. This is a beautiful area, lots of farmland with mountains in the distance in just about every direction. Although it's currently out of sight, the river we've been following isn't far from town.

"Okay, everyone," Rey says, motioning us to stop, "stay sharp. We have no reason to believe there will be any trouble, but this wide-open space makes the hair on the back of my neck stand up. Kimba, you'll keep the group back here, while Atticus and I make contact at the roadblock."

Set perpendicular to the road is a line of bumper-to-bumper cars stretching well into the field on either side, providing an effective and efficient barrier. It's also the only good use of new-model cars that were rendered useless by the EMP. In the middle of the road are several more cars parked at slight angles. The space in front of the cars has been scraped clear of any snow, showing bare pavement. The road beyond is just like the man in Belfry said: the highway's plowed clear of snow as far as I can see.

A man holds up his hand and waves us forward. "C'mon over."

Rey looks to Kimba, who answers with a shrug. "All right. Let's all go. Nice and slow."

"Hello, folks." The man holds up his hand in greeting, his tactical rifle on the hood of the car next to him. There are a few others, all armed, using cars as protection. "Welcome to Bridger. We're happy to have you pass through. The road from here until the other side of Fromberg is controlled access and requires a toll collection."

"Thank you," Rey answers in his American voice. "We heard about the toll, but what's the controlled access mean?"

"Just that we'll ask you to stay on the main road. You won't be able to stop in town—either here or Fromberg. We've cleared the road to make travel easier."

"What about camping?"

"Not a problem as long as you stay in designated areas. There's one here." He points to a cleared space not far from the barricade with two portable toilets. "We've also set up a spot on the other side of Bridger and another a little farther down the road, an old rest stop. Just don't use the toilets in the buildings—we've set up outhouses. Plus there's a couple more areas before you reach Fromberg. No dispersed camping, only the established campgrounds."

He looks at our group, making eye contact with most of us. "We've set up latrines and recycling bins so you can keep things neat and tidy. And you're welcome to use the latrine here should you have a need at the moment." He points again at the portable toilet.

I make a face, imagining just how bad that blue box might be.

"And your horses," he continues, "beautiful animals. We'll ask you clean up after them. Keep the road tidy. You'll find compost stations next to the recycling bins. Nothing gets wasted these days, you know. You have any trouble with the wagon? Or sled . . . whatever it is."

"No trouble at all," PJ answers, still perched on his wagon seat. "They're a good team. We don't push them too hard."

"I meant with bandits."

Rey stiffens. "Meaning?"

"Just wondering. We used to hear about cars being targets, but we haven't seen a vehicle come through in ages. But there were issues before the weather took hold. There's been a few other teams through here, but it's pretty rare. We have a couple in the community. We're all pretty blessed we were living in small places like this. I can't even imagine what it's like in the cities. Sounds like Billings is bad enough. 'Course, the president says they're starting with the cities to get them fixed up. Guess he knows we can keep taking care of ourselves while they set those hooligans straight."

"That sounds about right." Rey smirks.

While Rey talks with the man, Beth and I remove our skis, setting them in the back of the wagon. We won't need them on the scraped ground. Soon, everyone has their skis off and is enjoying the feeling of freedom.

After wrapping up the conversation with the barricade greeter, Rey motions to PJ, who hops down from the wagon and grabs a burlap bag out of the back. We've already prepared our toll: a plucked goose wrapped in a piece of muslin, with the feathers in a separate well-worn plastic bag, plus an already cooked haunch of venison, compliments of Scruff. We also have a few sugar beets, part of the rations given to us by the mountain community for our travels. Sugar beets have been one of our main food sources after a decent harvest last fall. I'm not a fan, but they've kept us alive.

There was some serious opposition to what a few considered a much too generous toll. While no one was terribly upset about giving up sugar beets—seems I'm not the only one who isn't a fan—Leanne was practically hysterical over the meat. She made it clear we wouldn't be giving food away if we'd watched our children slowly starve to death. Her antics got Donnie and even Robyn in her corner.

While I understand Donnie taking her position, especially after finding out about their little romance, Robyn surprised me. Leanne is never nice to her, not that she's nice to anyone. Why side with her? Even Icky Vicky seemed to be swayed by Leanne's argument.

In the end, she was overruled, but there was plenty of drama. And there's still hard looks being passed around. Sometimes, I feel like I'm in kindergarten with little kids getting in playground squabbles. But at the same time, I can understand Leanne's concerns.

She and her family still have several weeks of travel ahead of them. Right now, we're in an area where the geese and wildlife are plentiful, thanks to the river we've been following and the many open fields and farmland. But that could certainly change. Maybe the guy who gave boiled snow had it right.

"Much obliged for your generous payment," the gate keeper says. "But we'll let you keep the beets."

Rey lets out a hearty laugh. "You have your fill of them?"

"This is sugar beet country. And we're grateful for them, but yeah, we have enough. We're good on geese too. It's been a banner year for them, more than I've ever seen, but we'll be happy to keep the one you're offering. We're preserving as much meat as we can for summer since we won't have the flyers then. They'll migrate out of here. We can't really believe how many we've had this year. I mean, with the weather and all, it seems with all the snow they'd find warmer places. Some of us have been talking, wondering if the bombs that went off are part of the reason we have so many geese."

"Could be." PJ stokes his beard. "We've definitely had some good goose hunting years in the past, but this is spectacular. We've been blessed. How's the deer?"

"Moderate. We're competing with the wolves for them. I'm not sure we're winning."

"We heard a couple of wolves last night." PJ motions toward me. "Tamra said she thought there's a sanctuary here?"

"Over there." The man motions to the western hillside. "Used to be, anyway. The owners . . . " He shakes his head. "They couldn't bear to put 'em down, so they opened the gates and let them go."

"Told you so," Donnie mutters under his breath.

"I wish they would've consulted the rest of us before they did that. It caused us some serious troubles." The man shakes his head.

"What're you doing?" Rey asks.

"About the wolves? They're shoot on sight."

A deep frown crosses my face. I get it. The wolves are amazing and beautiful creatures, and while not a direct threat to the people living here, the food competition is real.

"Well, folks, there's another group coming up behind you, so I'll let you get on your way."

I turn and look behind us. A ragtag bunch about half the size of ours is several hundred yards away.

"Don't worry about rushing through town, but please do use the facilities here if you can't wait until you reach the other side," the man says, again pointing to the porta potties. "From this gate to the next latrine is just under a mile and a half. We've set up the old Maverik gas station as a rest stop. There's a stop every mile and a half or so until you reach Fromberg."

"One more thing," I say, stepping closer to the man. "When we reach Fromberg, we want to take the Joliet Fromberg Road. Will that be a problem?"

"Shouldn't be. Just let them know at their roadblock where you're going. Last I heard, they're escorting people until they reach the other side of town. My guess is they'll get you outside of town and let you be. That'll save some miles if you're heading west. Where're you folks planning to end up?"

"A variety of places," Rey answers, while I proudly exclaim, "I'm from Joliet."

"You are, huh? Well then, welcome home."

"And she's the only reason we're going that way," Leanne says in her snottiest voice. "We're making a special detour just for her."

I guess it was too much to hope we might have made a truce after she asked me to keep her secret.

"That's right nice of you," the greeter answers with a slight hesitation to his voice. "It's always good to have friends watching out for you."

"Humph." Leanne throws over her shoulder as she stomps toward the toilets.

I let out a sigh as Rey pats me on the arm. "Don't worry about her."

"I try not to."

We move away from the blockade to the wide area and the toilets. The campground is set up just to the south of the bathrooms. There's a couple of sections of lodge pole pine fashioned into old-style hitching posts. PJ tends to the team, giving them sips from a bucket and face rubs, while Kimba and Rey stand near him with their heads close together.

Leanne was in and out of the bathroom quickly, shooting me a look on her way by. Others from our party take their turn, as I wait by the hitching post and watch the younger children begin a game of tag, taking advantage of the open space and their break from the wagon.

The older girls, along with Robyn, plop down on several logs that double as seating near where the Bridger greeter is. He carries on a conversation with them while he awaits the next group. He must say something funny, because Beth gives a hearty laugh.

Leading his horse, Donnie eases up to the group standing by the team. I'm near enough I overhear when he quietly says, "I think we ought to keep an eye on those guys." He lifts his chin toward the group that's only steps away from the barricade. "There's only a couple of rough-looking women, and no children, with half a dozen dudes."

Rey's eyes scour the group. "Eight dudes, actually. Everyone on a swivel."

"Howdy, folks," the Bridger man says, raising his hand to the new people.

I open my mouth to call for Beth to come over to the toilet as a single gunshot echoes through the open space. I watch in horror as a bead of blood appears dead center on the greeter's forehead. It's immediate chaos as those standing behind the barricade return fire.

"Beth! Debbie!" I yell, taking two steps toward them before I'm knocked to the ground.

"Get down!" someone yells.

"My children!"

"Just wait," one of the A Boys whispers. "Just wait. You can't help them if you're dead."

The shooting stops after a voice calls out, "I have hostages. You should listen to our terms, and we will reach an amicable agreement."

Looking for the voice, I flash back to a few weeks ago when the safety of our mountain retreat was shattered during a wedding by Victoria Dawson's husband and accomplices. They took several of the community children hostage.

Now a stranger with matted hair is holding on to Kimba's teenage daughter. He has his arm around her neck and a gun to her head, as he crouches on one side of the barrier, out of sight of the defending forces from Bridger. Leanne's daughter and Robyn are held by two other men.

I quickly scan for Beth, my breath coming in short bursts as the panic fills me. *Where is she?* Where's Debbie and the other children?

"Do you see my daughters?" I whisper, hoping someone around me will answer.

"Everyone stay where you are," Rey says in a harsh whisper. "We'll figure this out. Kimba, slowly make your way to me, love."

As Rey is giving us instructions, someone from the Bridger brigade calls out, "You're hopelessly outnumbered and have nothing to negotiate with."

"Perhaps you didn't hear me," the abductor replies. "We have hostages, two young girls and a pretty woman. Do you want their blood on your hands?"

"What do you want?" a new voice from Bridger asks.

"What everyone wants! Food, medicine— " He looks toward us, taking the gun from his hostage's head and waving it in our direction. "And those horses and wagon. That'll do for a start."

I hear PJ muttering under his breath, as Rey whispers, "Atticus, as soon as his eyes aren't on you, start moving south in a flanking position. Take your brothers. Nice and slow. You know what to do. Be ready for the show."

As the back and forth between the attackers and the defenders continues, I scour the area for Beth or Debbie.

Catching movement by the wagon wheel, I see Leanne's son. When he sees me looking at him, he moves slightly and shows me that

Debbie's pressed to the ground with the young Hoffmann girl next to her. Tiny, skinny, malnourished Sebastian Monroe is doing his best to provide a shield, covering his friends and keeping them safe.

I give him a nod as tears fill my eyes.

Closing my eyes and taking a deep breath, I try and remember the scene before everything went crazy. They were sitting on the logs. Those now held hostage were closest to the man who was murdered. Beth was at the far end.

My eyes dart to the fourth log seat, then continue past two more logs where the makeshift seating arrangement ends. The final log is nestled against the wheel of a green minivan.

Next to the minivan is a little commuter car of some sort. I concentrate on the space between the two vehicles. The snow's been scraped off in the greeting area and around the log seats to the edge of the bumper-to-bumper cars. The ground between the cars is snow covered, but not terribly, thanks to the way they're compacted together.

As I'm watching, the snow seems to move and then I see a flash of black. I take in a deep breath. She's still in her skinning boots, we all are. Hers are black with white bottoms. *Please, please let it be Beth. And please let her be okay.*

I let out a long, slow breath as I again focus on the hostage takers. As Rey said, there's eight men and two women. All are about the same level of filth and shabbiness, which isn't unexpected in this world.

Only two in the group have snowshoes, while the rest are wearing various styles of boots, many with some kind of cleats or spikes attached to help with traction. The ones with snowshoes are bent over, removing them.

The older woman glowers at one of the guys taking off his snowshoes and then gives him a kick, knocking him on his bottom.

The younger woman, sporting dreadlocks with twigs that appear to have been purposely placed and is wearing a pink tutu over her snow clothes, gives a harsh laugh. "Guess Mama told you, didn't she? Dummy."

In minuscule increments, I remove the Scout strapped to my three-point Ching sling until it's hanging off, then quietly set it on the ground. We're too close for the rifle to be the smart choice.

As soon as it's on the ground, just as slowly, I unholster my sidearm and keep it by my thigh. Unlike that night when I was on watch in

Bakerville and didn't think about pulling my weapon, today I'm going to be ready. The training we've been doing has left me much more confident.

A quick glance at Rochelle, who's now crouched at the edge of the toilet on the left with the wagon between her and the bad guys, shows she also has her weapon at the ready. She gives me a shake of her head and motions for me to stay put. I have no intentions of doing anything foolish. I just plan to be ready for the show—whatever Rey meant by that—and making sure my children are safe.

PJ's with the horses, crouched slightly and holding on to them with one hand, his pistol in the other. Donnie's horse is also with PJ, but not Donnie. I'm surprised the horses didn't bolt when the shooting happened. PJ said they've been around shooting all their lives, but this was a shootout—way different than shooting at an elk or deer.

And what about Donnie's horse? He seems the calmest of the bunch. The two horses with the team look nervous, flicking their ears back and forth. The one I can see fully is standing slightly splay legged, looking like he's considering fleeing.

"Whoa, you're okay." PJ's voice is soft and gentle. The team is bent at a jack-knife angle from the wagon. When one of the horses moves slightly, my view of Debbie is completely blocked.

As I move so I can see my daughter, I hear a sing-song voice call out, "Excuse me!"

Chapter 18

"Hi there!" Kimba waves and smiles.

In the few minutes since I've seen her, she's taken her long blond hair out of the braid hanging down her back and removed her stocking cap. Her locks now glisten in the morning sun, with the light breeze teasing and lifting her tresses. She's removed her parka and even unzipped her hooded sweater.

As she waves, she glides forward like a model on the catwalk. "I think I can help. I mean, if you *want* my help." Her voice is inviting. Sultry.

The guy holding Kimba's daughter gives a big smile as his eyes bug out. "Well, hello, honey. Where'd you come from?"

The other guys in the group all have some sort of reaction—catcalls or some disgusting reply. The two women swing their weapons, training them on Kimba.

Kimba giggles like a schoolgirl.

I can't help but roll my eyes. These guys can't really be that stupid, can they?

"Oh, I was just over there," Kimba answers in her ultra-feminine timbre. "I was using the little girl's room when I heard all the ruckus. You said you need some medicine? Are you hurt? I was a candy striper, and I can probably make you feel better."

"Oh, I bet you can. Mm-hmm," he says, while several of the other guys make some sort of disgusting remark.

Okay, yep. They *are* that stupid.

With another giggle, she flips her hair and says in a playful voice, "It's so easy to just drop to the ground."

"Mm-hmm, baby, it sure is," he says.

The old woman scoffs while the tutu wearer asks, "What's that supposed to mean?"

"Oh, nothing much," Kimba says, giving her hair another flip. "I was just talking to the other women."

"The other women?" someone asks. "What women?"

"Drop! Now!" Kimba yells as both hands come forward, her pistol in perfect shooter's position.

Kimba's daughter dissolves like a wet noodle; the man, suitably distracted by *the show*, is unable to hold on to her. Out of the corner of my eye, I see the other two also go to the ground.

The old lady yells while popping off a shot. Several more gunshots sound out.

I bite my lip to keep from letting out a yell of my own as I shrink into the ground, keeping my eyes on what's happening. Even though I'm confident with my pistol when shooting at targets, and the drills and dryfire training we've been doing have given me confidence, I'm not combat trained. And that's what this is: combat.

Backing away from the fight, while firing her handgun toward the roadblock, is the younger tutu-wearing woman. The older woman's by her side. She says something to her, causing the tutu wearer to stop.

Tutu lady looks toward the wagon—where Debbie and the other children are hiding. She swivels and yells something undistinguishable, but I understand at my core.

She's going to shoot the children.

Moving to one knee, I quickly bring my weapon to bear. Like in practice, when PJ tapped my shoulder, I fire off four quick rounds.

She falls to the ground like a lump.

My stomach flips.

The old woman yells and aims her weapon at me.

I swivel to shoot again. Before I can pop off another shot, she falls to the ground, her pistol skittering away.

"Report!" Rey yells as the shooting stops.

"I'm hit," someone calls out. Is it Scruff? There are cries and screams of pain coming from all around.

Scrambling to my feet, Rochelle says, "Wait, Tamra. Stay where you are until we get the all clear."

"My children!" I cry.

"Just wait."

Doesn't anyone understand the urgency of making sure our children are safe?

I sidestep to the left, clearing the hitching post and drilling my gaze toward the wagon wheel.

I still can't see. I take another shuffle left.

"Tamra," Rochelle hisses.

I wave her off and shuffle again. *There!*

The girls are on the ground, with Sebastian still positioned to protect them. Debbie's head is turned in my direction. Seeing me, she starts to cry. Sebastian pats her on the back. I give her a smile and mouth, "*You're okay.*"

She nods and lifts a thumb.

Now Beth. Where is she?

My left movement becomes right movement as I scoot in the direction of the roadblock. I've gone less than a yard when Kimba calls out, "We're clear."

Everything is a whirlwind as people appear out of nowhere, everyone suddenly moving.

It's pandemonium.

I take off running toward where I thought I saw Beth's boot. As soon as I reach the small space between the minivan and the commuter car, I drop to my knees.

Nothing! No boot. No Beth.

Standing, I twist my body, frantically searching.

"Mom!"

I yank my head around.

"Here! I'm here!" She's waving from behind one of the cars about fifty yards from the roadblock.

"She's fine, ma'am," a lady nearby says. "Let's get your injured taken care of."

My reunion with my children is amazing. As I hold them both close, Debbie keeps repeating how scared she was. Beth agrees. I tell them over and over how impressed I am with their quick thinking and getting to safety. Beth responds with a classic young-teen eye roll but does give a courtesy, "Thanks, Mom."

"Is he . . . is he dead?" Leanne asks, her voice a hoarse whisper.

My breath catches. She and Rey are kneeling next to a body.

Donnie.

"He's breathing," Rey answers. "But I don't know how."

"What happened?" Debbie asks.

Rey lifts his head to meet her gaze. "Maybe you and your mom can help Robyn? She's injured."

"We will," I say, moving Debbie away from Donnie. I give him a quick glance. The side of Donnie's head is covered in blood.

Closer to the wagon, PJ and Rochelle are kneeling by Scruff. Rochelle's holding his hand while PJ wraps a bandage around his leg.

There're bodies everywhere . . . the tutu-wearing lady I shot, the men.

Kimba and Victoria are working on one man. Jennifer and one of her boys are next to the old lady who, though injured, is cussing up a storm. And she's making plenty of threats about how we're going to pay for what we've done.

"Keep your eyes on the ground, girls," I whisper. "Don't . . . you don't need to look around."

"I've seen dead people before," Debbie whispers back. "Remember— "

"I don't want to remember," Beth says harshly. "You shouldn't either."

The girls and I make our way to Robyn, sitting on one of the upturned logs.

"Are you okay?" I ask.

"My shoulder. Hurts . . . something awful."

"What happened?"

"Something went wrong when I was trying to drop to the ground. It wasn't as easy as Kimba made it sound." Robyn gives me a weak smile. "I heard a pop. That can't be good, right?"

Within a few minutes, Donnie and Scruff are being carried away on board stretchers. PJ asks Robyn if she wants to ride in the wagon, but she decides getting in it would be more painful than walking.

We follow to, what was before our world fell apart, an abandoned building across the street from the old grocery store. It's now set up as the medical clinic. While our injured are taken inside, the rest of us are instructed to sit at tables and benches on the sidewalk.

"Donnie?" I ask.

"Doesn't look good." Kimba shakes her head.

"He'll be fine," Leanne interjects, wringing her hands.

"Maybe so," Rey says. "Let's pray, not only for Donnie but for Scruff and Robyn too."

Leanne steps away as the rest of us move closer together and bow our heads. I'm surprised to see Leanne's daughter stays with us. Usually, she'll avoid prayer or Bible study like her mom. Victoria and her youngest son, who are lukewarm at best in all things religious, also stay.

To be fair, I'm lukewarm, too, but I find it's easier just to join in than make a stink about it. As long as they're not preaching at me, like

Kimba tried to this morning, I'm fine. If it gets too weird, I'll just walk away.

"PJ?" Rey asks. "Would you mind?"

As is his way, PJ uses plain and sincere language as he asks God to help our friends. He barely has the amen out of his mouth when the door of the makeshift clinic opens. It's the same lady who I'd briefly spoken to at the roadblock, the one who told me Beth was fine.

"They're taking care of your friends," she says.

"Do you know anything yet?" the younger Dawson boy asks.

"No, sorry."

"Where should we go?" Kimba asks. "To the campground?"

"I've been told to take you to one of our vacant houses. We're grateful for your help in stopping the attack."

"Are your people okay?"

She lets out a sigh and shakes her head. "We lost two, including the one you were talking to. Four severely injured. A few minor injuries."

The lady walks us to a little house a few blocks away. Leanne leads Donnie's horse while PJ handles the team and wagon.

"The yard's big enough for the horses," she says. "There's two houses and the garage. Both are small but should be enough room for all of you."

"Have you all thought of putting a few snipers outside the barrier, setting up a crossfire?" Kimba asks. "And don't have your man out in the open like that. This isn't the SuperMart where you need someone welcoming them to your town."

"We didn't . . . we thought it'd be best if we made it clear we aren't a threat."

"How'd that work out?" Kimba asks softly. "You've got a good start here. You just need to do some tweaking."

About an hour later, after we've settled into the two houses and are all gathered in the largest house for lunch, a man arrives with Robyn, her arm in a sling.

"They don't think it's broken," she says. "Maybe dislocated."

"We still want to treat it like it's broken," the man says. "Limit your motion, and take it easy."

"Donnie?" Leanne asks, her voice cracking on his name.

"The one with the leg wound? Or the head?"

"Head."

"That's a miracle for sure. He's still out cold, but the bullet only grazed him—furrowed a path all the way to the bone above his temple." He makes a motion across his head, showing us. "Truly a miracle. As long as he wakes up, he should be fine."

"As long as he wakes up," Leanne echoes.

"Yeah. He, um, he could be in a coma. Maybe. We don't really know for sure, so it's a matter of wait and see."

"Brilliant," Leanne scoffs. "What kind of doctors do you have here?"

"Um . . . no doctors. We have a veterinarian and a nurse. The rest of us, we just do the best we can. And the other guy, he'll be okay too. The bullet caught the meaty part of his calf. He's not going to be up and around anytime soon, but after a few weeks . . . " He finishes with a shrug.

"Is that what your vet thinks?" Leanne asks, narrowing her eyes.

"When can we see them?" Rey asks.

"Maybe tomorrow. There's a storm coming in, so we're battening down the hatches. I heard you all might have some ideas to help our security issues. Would you be able to meet with our town council and give us some guidance?"

"We could do that," Rey says. "When?"

"After the storm passes. This is the second time we've been attacked. We got lucky the first time, no one died. Today . . . " He lets out a long breath. "Today is hard. Two are dead so far and one more that we're not sure will make it. We aren't sure the male attacker will make it either, but the woman—she'll be fine. Boy, has she got a mouth on her."

"What'll you do with her?"

"Treating her, then we'll get her secured."

"You have a jail?"

"We did. It was just a holding facility, but we lost that last summer when—well, it doesn't matter what happened. We'll make sure she's secure."

After the man leaves, the girls and I snuggle into a nest of blankets we've arranged on the floor near the blazing woodstove. I listen as they each replay the day's events, working on releasing their anxieties and fears.

"Sebastian said you shot the lady with the tutu." Debbie leans her head against my shoulder. "He said she might have shot us if you didn't get her first."

My eyes fill with tears, and my heart pounds at the memory of shooting the woman and watching her fall like a lump to the ground.

I know it was a clean shot, quick and life ending. The life-ending part is what's giving me pause. I did what was needed. When she turned the gun toward the children, the choice was made for me.

I just wish I'd stop reliving it each time I close my eyes. And I wish my stomach would stop doing flip-flops.

"Kimba said Mom's a hero," Beth says. "She did the right thing."

"I know she's a hero," Debbie says. "She'll always do anything to keep us safe."

Chapter 19

I shot and killed the tutu wearer two days ago. I still remember how she dropped. It replays over and over in my head. While I don't think I actually heard the sound of her hitting the ground, my mind has now added a thump. At least now the sick feeling to my stomach isn't as bad.

We're still at the house in Bridger, where we've been waiting out a storm that came barreling in with mass amounts of snow and zero-degree temperatures.

Being so close to my parents in Joliet, yet stuck and unable to reach them, is hard. Leaving the mountain in the middle of March should've put us there well before now. But with the weather and other delays, and now this shootout . . . I let out a sigh.

The two houses the town gave us to use have worked out well. Neither are very big, but each has a woodstove, which not only keeps the small houses warm but are suitable for cooking. We've divided up, putting the older boys and men in one house and the women and children in the other. Kimba's son, Nate, was ecstatic to be included in the men's house.

With only two bedrooms, my girls and I are rooming with Leanne and her children—not my choice. Even with being in the small town of Bridger, we're still keeping watch, having one person in each house and using the radio to stay in contact.

Donnie woke up sometime in the middle of the night after getting shot, confused and disoriented by his surroundings, and not recognizing anyone in Bridger's medical clinic.

One of the workers in their makeshift clinic soon came pounding on our door to see if we could help. The noise woke up those of us not on watch, and Leanne, who I don't think had been sleeping anyway, insisted she would go.

As she was getting ready, I heard her whispering to her daughter. Whatever she said must not have gone over well since it garnered a huff from the girl. I felt myself smile. Leanne's daughter is always so quiet and well behaved. I was beginning to think she was anything but a typical adolescent.

Before Leanne left the room, she turned to me and said, "Um, I'd appreciate it if you'd care for my children should—well, can you keep an eye out for them?"

Leanne asking *me* for help? Weird. I'm sure the surprise was evident in my voice as I assured her I would.

Donnie was released the next day. I've yet to see him. He's been in the other house nursing a massive headache. Leanne and her children go back and forth as much as the weather allows, visiting and checking on him. Rumor is, when he's not sleeping, he's complaining or grouching.

Kimba keeps him as medicated as she can, having used all of the narcotics and most of the lighter painkillers. We know it means there'll be nothing for later use, but what can be done? The man was shot in the head!

Robyn's arm is taped to her side to keep her from moving it. Even so, the pain is still intense at times. Kimba offered her OTC meds, but she refused, insisting Donnie needed them more. She's alternating heat and ice to control the pain. The small, dark bottle smells like booze and is made from one of the trees growing along the river. The storm has been good in a way, giving them extra time to heal before we hit the road.

When we do leave, hopefully in the next day or two, Scruff will be staying behind. The bullet tore through the muscle and left considerable damage and weakness.

He's still in the makeshift hospital but will be moved to a house with a few other single men and allowed time to recuperate. Even though he wasn't with us for long, I already miss his easy and comforting ways.

Before the worst of the storm, a couple of our people went out with a group of Bridger residents to hunt geese. They brought home four for us, which were cut into meat strips and are being dried on wire behind the continuously burning woodstove. They also added several to the Bridger food supply as a thank you for tending to our wounded and allowing us time to recuperate and wait out the storm before moving on.

We're taking advantage of the downtime and ramping up the weapon and self-defense training. Using the garage as our training studio, Kimba went over basic escape moves, things like Robyn and the girls used when Kimba told them to drop.

Although Robyn was injured in the maneuver, she's still alive. Kimba insists it was a success, while offering additional tips to avoid injury in similar situations.

In addition to group drills and training, Kimba or Rey are also taking time to work with people like me one on one—those of us who are a lot less proficient. I'm amazed by the things I'm learning, even without being able to actually shoot live bullets. I'm especially enjoying the tips on how to draw my weapon from its holster.

Every time we practice, I feel my confidence increase. Not that I ever want to have to use my gun again, but at least now I feel like I can. I shake my head, remembering the night only a short while ago when I didn't even think about pulling my pistol after hearing a shot.

When we aren't practicing self-defense, we're talking, reading, or playing games while waiting out the storm. I spend a lot of time visiting with Kimba, Jennifer, and Rochelle. To my surprise, I've even talked with Leanne a few times. Nothing deep or meaningful, and she's still not a pleasant person, but at least she isn't snapping at me.

I've been thinking a lot about my conversation with Kimba in those early morning hours of guard duty when she told me about becoming a Christian. Even though at the time I felt like she was preaching at me, trying to convince me of something I had no interest in, the more I think about her story, the more I want to know.

As the four of us sit at the kitchen table playing a hand of rummy, I nervously ask, "What made you want to be a Christian?"

"Me?" Kimba asks.

"You. All of you, really. Kimba, you said you heard about the Gospel, but was that it?" I ask, looking to the three women. "I know a little about why Rochelle did—you know, with how bad things were for her, she thought maybe God could make things easier."

Rochelle lets out a snort of laughter. "Not exactly. It wasn't that long ago when God didn't matter to me. Then I began to understand who I was. And who He is. That's when I realized how much I needed Him."

"You needed Him for what?" I ask. "To feel better?"

"Not to feel better but to *be* better, to live the right kind of life."

"Then you can earn a spot into heaven," I say, nodding.

"Not earn." Jennifer smiles. "God doesn't look at the things we've done and decide if we belong in heaven. He looks at our faith. Trusting in Christ is the only way we can have eternal life."

Rochelle and Kimba bob their heads.

"Oh, yeah, sure." I feel the crimson travel up my cheeks. "I, uh, I know about that, about needing to believe in God."

"Though that is necessary," Jennifer says, "it's more than just believing there is a God. We need to believe we're loved and accepted by Him."

"Okay."

"And we need to acknowledge our sinful nature." Jennifer gives me a smile. "That's the hard part for some. It was for me. I knew I was a good person, always going out of my way to help others. Sure, I may have thought about things . . . sinful things. But I rarely acted on them. But as I got to know God, I realized even thinking about sin is . . . well, it's sin. I was good by my standards, but I wasn't good by God's standards. God looks at hatred as murder, at lust as adultery."

"Hatred as murder? I doubt that." The memory of tutu lady hitting the ground plays through my head.

"It's in the Bible," Rochelle says quietly. "Anyone who hates a brother or sister is a murderer. It's in . . . " She looks to Jennifer.

"First John," Jennifer answers. "That was another hard one. Even though I was nice to most people, there were some . . . oh, they'd make me nuts, some in my own family even."

"Is that why you do the Golden Rule thing?" I ask, thinking of my name calling. While I've never really come up with the nicknames to be truly mean, is it the same? Am I as bad as a murderer? Is my little nickname game sinful?

"God has given me a heart to love." Jennifer's voice is soft, compassionate. "Once I learned about God and who He is—what love really is—it was easy to decide to love those who may seem like they don't deserve it. Along with that love, He's given me compassion, especially for those who are still lost, that they will seek and see the truth and then turn to Christ."

I stare at the cards in my hand. "I don't think I could do it. People have been terrible to me. How can I love them? When people are cruel, how can I show them love? I want to . . . I want to be cruel right back."

"When we know and experience God's love for ourselves," Jennifer says, "we want to share the love with others. It changes everything."

A new day dawns bright and clear. The storm has finally stopped, and we're making plans to leave. Robyn and Donnie each insist they're feeling okay—at least well enough to make the journey. And it's not a moment too soon. We've all had enough of being cooped up.

Several of us are sitting at the table in the small kitchen, working on boning out a few geese brought down this morning, when I hear Debbie cry, "Give that back!"

"Make me," a deep voice responds.

I lift my head to glance at Victoria. She doesn't even look up, just keeps her focus on her goose. Setting my knife down with a thump, I slide my chair out and step into the living room.

Jameson Dawson, the younger of Victoria's boys, is holding a coloring book up in the air. Debbie jumps for it, but he lifts it higher, just out of her reach.

"Stop being mean to her," Leanne's son says, standing tall, hands balled into fists.

"Make me, twerp," Jameson challenges.

"Enough!" I lift my hand in a stop motion. "Stop picking on the little kids."

"You're not the boss of me." Jameson folds his arms across his chest.

"Maybe not, but Debbie is my child. Leave her alone."

"Don't talk to my son that way!" Victoria bounds out of the kitchen.

I shake my head at her. "He's being a bully and is picking on the younger children. Can you talk to him?"

"Don't you dare tell me what to do." She wags her finger at me while Jameson gives me a haughty look.

"Hey," I say, raising my hands, "your son needs to realize he can't pick on the younger kids. And if you aren't going to— "

"My son is mine to reprimand. Worry about your own whiny brat and there won't be a problem."

"My what?" I ask, raising my voice.

Kimba steps in. "Victoria, Jameson was out of line. He was purposely picking on the younger children."

Victoria starts to sputter as Jameson clenches his fists.

"I get we're all tired of being cooped up in here." Kimba's voice is full of patience. "With the storm letting up, we'll get going soon. But until then, there's no more of this. Got it, Jameson?"

"Let's go." Victoria tugs her son's arm and gives Kimba a look of pure hatred as they make their way to the back bedroom.

I give Kimba a grateful look before going to Debbie. Once she's calm, I return to my work in the kitchen. A short while later, the men from the other house show up for lunch.

"Where's my mom?" Brett Dawson asks, looking for Victoria.

"She's— " I start.

"Jameson was picking on Debbie," Kimba says quickly. "There was a little thing. Everything's okay now. Can you tell her and your brother lunch is ready?"

With a frown and a nod, he goes into the bedroom. We're serving lunch when shouts fill the small house. It's not difficult to hear the words being used as both Jameson and Victoria berate the older boy. A few minutes later, Brett rushes through the living room, his cheeks red and his eyes down. He goes out the door without a word to anyone.

When Victoria and Jameson make their way to the kitchen a short while later, Jameson glares at me, as if daring me to say something.

Taking a deep breath, I square my shoulders. While I'd like to give him a big piece of my mind, I try Jennifer's approach of kindness and love. I don't feel any bit of either toward Jameson or his mom, but even so, I give him a smile. "The stew's still warm."

His face softens as he bobs his head. "Thanks. It smells good."

Chapter 20

"I need to get out of here for a bit, take the girls for a walk or something," I say to Rochelle. "These walls are closing in, and I can't imagine another day trapped inside."

"I'm with you on that. PJ and I are going to take the horses out, get them a little exercise. They've been cooped up too long also. Want to walk with us?"

"I'm thinking I might take them to that park PJ was telling us about—plenty of room to run around."

Rochelle glances at Beth, deep in conversation with Nicole Hoffmann. Leanne's daughter Sadie is sitting nearby, trying to look uninterested but still hanging on to every word, as the more dynamic girls chat. Sadie is terribly quiet. I'm sure I haven't heard her utter more than a dozen words in the time we've been on our journey. She's quiet, but at least she's pleasant—definitely not like her mom.

Since that morning I walked up on Leanne and Donnie, she's been better toward me, maybe only making nice so I don't spill the beans about their relationship. I don't mind! I know we aren't friends, but I like her not going out of her way to grouch at me.

She's been so concerned with Donnie recovering from his injuries, the shot to his hand and the new shot to his head, she hasn't really taken the time to cause trouble with any of us. We've all noticed a change in her, and I don't think her romance is a secret to anyone now.

"Maybe just Debbie and I'll go."

"Probably a good idea," Rochelle answers. "She seems completely engrossed in whatever they're talking about."

Fifteen minutes later, bundled against the cold air, not only Debbie and I but also Sebastian and Kimba's youngest child, Naomi, make our way out of the house to a park a few blocks away.

The town has already been out clearing the city streets, scraping the newest snowfall to make it passable. Although the main road through town is plowed the full width, the side streets have trails for walking and driving quads. To the side of the plowed trail is a track where a snowmobile or two have been.

"Thanks for taking us to play, Mrs. Nicholson," Sebastian says as we approach the playground.

"We should build a snowman!" Debbie exclaims.

"Yes!" Naomi pumps her fist in the air.

"Two snowmen!" Sebastian shouts.

I resist the urge to ask how they can even want to play in the snow after almost six months of it being on the ground. But actual play isn't something they've had time to do since we left the safety of the mountain. No snowmen, no snow angels, no snowball fights. Just trudging along day in and day out—or, in the case of these three youngest of our group, riding in the wagon. It's less physically taxing but no more exciting.

As the children laugh and play in the snow, I feel almost normal, like this is just a regular wintry day we can enjoy. For a few minutes, the changes to our world, to our life, are not at the forefront of my mind.

The four of us are lying side by side, flapping our arms and legs in the snow, making angels, when a voice asks, "Hey, what are you doing out here?"

I lift myself onto an elbow to address two men staring at us. "You know, snow angels?"

"Right. I mean, didn't you hear about the trouble and staying inside?" the larger of the two asks.

"What trouble?" I get to my feet and motion the children to do the same.

"Oh! Hey, are you with that group passing through?" the other one asks. "I bet they forgot to tell 'em." He nudges the other guy.

"Tell us what?" I ask.

"Those two that attacked us, they escaped."

"Escaped? How?" I pull Debbie close to one side of me and Naomi to the other. "Sebastian, step over here."

"The old woman got out of her restraints, knocked out our guy watching her and took his firearms. Then she got the man loose and injured the nurse on duty."

"I thought . . . wasn't he seriously injured?"

"Yeah. But they still got away. You all should get back to the house. Tell your people to be on alert."

"Yes, okay. When did this happen?"

"Close to daylight. They tied up our people. We found them when a new shift went in at eight."

"Let's go, kids." I motion toward the street.

"You want us to walk you back?" the larger of the two asks.

"You walk them back," the other one says. "I'm going to meet up with Kunz."

"Sounds good. I'll meet you at the old RV dump station."

"Don't be long."

"Yep." The man turns to me. "Let's go, ma'am."

As we get back on the plowed section of the road, the man says, "We're sure they're long gone. I mean, they'd be stupid not to take off. But we're still looking for them."

"Did you find their tracks in the snow?" Sebastian asks.

"Nothing outside of the scraped trails we made. Say . . . are you the one?"

"The one?" I ask.

"The one the old lady was going on about? The one who killed her daughter?"

My heart lurches to my throat. "I . . . uh . . . yes."

"Thought so. I've guarded her a few times. She was going on and on about the woman wearing the burnt orange stocking cap."

"I, um— " I lift my hand to my hat.

"She was cursing you and promising she'll make you pay."

"Make me pay? They attacked *us*!"

"Yeah, well . . . " He shrugs. "She's a few cards short of a full deck. There's no reasoning with someone like that. Why—Argh!" he screams as he grabs his leg.

The percussion of a rifle fills the silence of the morning.

"Move!" he yells, pulling his rifle to the front as he goes down on his uninjured knee.

"Go!" I yell to the children, motioning to a bunch of shrubbery at the edge of a yard.

"Y'all better just hold still now," the gravelly voice of a longtime smoker calls out. "My partner's got a perfect bead on that little blond kid. I'd hate to see such a pretty child covered in blood. Drop the rifle, tough guy."

"Mom?" Debbie asks.

"Wait," I whisper, unsure if she can even hear me over my pounding heart. "We're going to be okay," I add slightly louder.

"They'll be coming soon," the man whispers, as he sets his rifle on the ground with one hand while holding his thigh with the other. The snow around him is a sickening crimson.

"Why'd you put the rifle down?" I ask, my voice coming out in a pant.

"What'd you want me to do? Risk her shooting one of the kids? I've got my pistol. And everyone had to hear that shot. They'll be here soon."

"Wondered when I'd find you." The old lady steps out from the edge of a house, a bolt-action hunting rifle in her hand. "Been lookin' around. Heard them talking about the house they put y'all up in. 'Magine my surprise to see you playing in the park. 'Course, that guy there 'bout ruined my plans. No matter. We'll wrap this up and get a move on out of here."

"Why?" I ask, trying to keep the quiver out of my voice. "Why not just . . . why didn't you just leave when you escaped?"

"Good thinking," the injured man whispers. "Buy time."

"You, deary."

"Me?"

"You're the one who killed my daughter."

"I don't know what you mean. I've never— "

"I recognize your hat!"

Reaching my hand to my hat, I swallow the lump in my throat. "Someone traded me for this. Some people passing through. They left yesterday as soon as the storm broke."

"I told you I didn't recognize any of them," a male voice says. "Let's get out of here." The man steps out from his hiding spot. He looks awful, pale and shaking, holding a pistol with one hand with his other arm in a sling. He even has the gun turned sideways like this is some sort of bad gangster movie.

"She's the one!" the lady yells. "I got a good look at her that day. I'm sure of it."

"Please. I'm not whoever you're looking for. It isn't me."

"Oh yeah? You willin' to sacrifice one of those kids to try and make me believe you're not the one who shot my daughter?" She lifts the rifle up. "Which one gets their brains splattered all over the snow?"

"Wait!" I step in front of Naomi and shove Debbie behind me.

"Ah, the boy, huh?"

Between clenched teeth, I whisper, "Kids, when I say *now*, you hit the ground. Any chance you can get to your pistol in a hurry?" I ask the man. "Shoot the guy."

"Times up, deary." She raises the rifle.

"Now!" I scream, as I lift my jacket with my left hand and pull out my pistol. The snow poofs up to my left as I fire. Once, twice—I watch as she falls to the ground. Swiveling to where the man was, I look for him and find him curled in a fetal position. I jump when another shot sounds. I quickly pivot back to the old lady.

"She's down," the man announces.

"Stand down! Stand down!" someone yells from a house down the block. "Put your weapon on the ground."

"She's okay! She's with us!" the injured townsman yells.

"Weapon on the ground. Now!"

I waste no time putting my pistol down. Debbie throws herself at my legs. With tears streaming down her face, Naomi whispers, "We're okay. We're okay." Sebastian pats her on the back. I open my arms and pull all three children toward me.

Things are a blur as people come running at us from all directions.

"She's part of the traveling group," the man on the ground keeps repeating over and over.

I'm separated from the children, which causes Debbie to scream, kick, and cry. The man, already receiving medical care, tells them it's not necessary.

After a few minutes, someone I recognize as having shown up at the house we're staying in says, "She's with the group, just like Eric said."

I kneel down and let the children come to me again. As soon as Debbie's calmish, I kiss her forehead and then turn to Eric, the man who was shot. "Why'd she do that?" I ask.

"I told you, she's out of her mind—*was* out of her mind."

"But why didn't she just shoot us? Why . . . why have a big conversation about killing me?"

The man tending to Eric says, "I guess she never saw *Die Hard*."

"What?" I ask.

"You know, 'Next time you have a chance to kill someone, do it.' Then Bruce Willis says, 'Thanks for the advice,' and blows him away."

"I don't think that's quite how it goes." Eric shakes his head. "But, yeah, something like that. She wanted to make sure you knew who shot you, and why."

I give a nod as my gaze travels to where the man with her is now being hoisted off the ground. "Did you shoot him?" I ask Eric.

"Nope. By the time I got my gun out, he was already laying there like that."

"But you shot her?"

"Figured it was the least I could do, after you did all the hard stuff." He sucks in a loud breath. "Hey! That hurts."

"Yeah, I bet," the guy working on him says, then raises his voice, "Okay, let's get him on the stretcher and to the hospital."

"Will he be okay?" I ask.

"I'm fine," Eric insists.

"I don't think it's more than a flesh wound," someone says. "That lady was a terrible shot."

The medic gives a combination of a nod and a shrug. "He'll be fine. Are you or the children injured?"

I shake my head, then ask the children. They all assure me they're okay, just scared and ready to go home.

"I'll find an escort for you," the medic says, as a man and woman pick up Eric.

"Thanks for your quick thinking," Eric calls to me as he's hustled away.

Before they can find anyone to walk me home, Rey and Kimba show up along with Rochelle and Leanne. The parents make sure their children are unharmed, while Rochelle fawns over Debbie and me.

"You're okay?" she asks.

I begin to cry and shake my head. "Get me back to the house."

Chapter 21

"Ready to go?" Kimba asks, resting a hand on my shoulder.

"More than ready. I'm beginning to hate this town."

"Understandable. You've faced some difficult things. Did your ears stop ringing?"

As we were walking back from yesterday's shooting, I was suddenly dizzy and couldn't hear. I immediately bent over and threw up. The dizziness was so bad I could barely walk upright. Rochelle and Kimba helped me get home.

The dizziness subsided after a nap, but the ringing in my ears continued through the night. Kimba said it was probably a combination of adrenaline and the noise of my pistol's repercussion knocking me off kilter.

"It's better this morning. I'm ready to go."

As I finish my packing, my thoughts travel to Dallas. When I was feeling so bad yesterday, I wished for his arms around me. Longed for his arms. I hate that he's not with me, will never be with me again.

And now, I just need to be with my mom, have her hold me and let me grieve his death properly. Maybe she can even help me get pass the guilt I feel for quickly moving on to Jackson and practically shoving my wonderful memories of Dallas and our marriage aside.

I want to be able to smile when I think of Dallas, to remember the good times we had without dwelling on how rotten I feel about Jackson. Without a doubt, marrying him was a mistake.

Once we get all our packing done and are waiting for the men to finish putting their stuff together, Kimba says, "When I was reading the Bible last night, I found something I thought was fitting for this point in our journey."

I glance to Leanne, who gives a slight eye roll but doesn't move away from the group.

"It's from Deuteronomy," Kimba continues. "Be strong and courageous . . ." She pauses as she looks around the room, tears rimming her eyes. "That's what all of you are, strong and courageous. We all took a chance leaving the safety of the mountain. For most of us, we still have a long way to go, so we need to continue to be strong, to be courageous, to lean on the Lord. I know— ”

Kimba's gaze meets mine. "I know not all of you are believers. Or your faith has been shaken and now you're not sure where you stand." Kimba lets out a giggle. "Look at me, thinking I'm a preacher all the sudden. Anyway, let me finish reading the verse. Um, I'm going to start over since I went off on a little tangent there. 'Be strong and courageous. Do not be afraid or terrified because of them, for the Lord your God goes with you; He will never leave you nor forsake you.'"

As she continues to read, I realize, unlike that morning when we had sentry duty together and I felt she was preaching at me, this time it feels okay. Instead of preachy, I can feel the love she has, not only for me but for each of the women here—even for Leanne and Victoria, who both make loving them difficult.

I look at Jennifer, who's definitely the most loving of any of us, as she wraps an arm around Victoria's shoulder. Victoria's chin is on her chest. Is she crying?

Until I moved up to the mountain outside of Bakerville last fall, I'd never gone to church other than a few weddings and funerals. As a child, my parents weren't religious. They didn't fault anyone who was, but they were busy with their lives, and there was no time for church or God. Same with Dallas and his family, so the tradition of church going didn't start.

It's not like we were atheists or even agnostic. We were just nothing. I spent zero time thinking about church, religion, or God. Then, when Dallas died and the EMP struck, I thought about God but not in a good way. I was angry.

I bite my lip as my own eyes fill with tears. Has God been helping me? If so, why? I haven't done anything to invite Him to help me. Even though Kimba and the others have tried to share the Gospel with me, I haven't done what they've said I need to do to become a child of God. I'll admit, part of me—maybe even most of me—admires these women who seem to rely on God.

Rochelle went through terrible things, first when she watched her husband's murder, then when she and her daughters were taken hostage and sold to the highest bidder, and finally being forced to marry her abusive captor before she was able to escape his wrath. Such terrible things!

I've seen her at her worst, after her farce of a marriage to Fred Lassiter became known. She was broken, a mere shell of a woman. But now, as I look at her, she seems so filled with peace.

Jennifer, whose kindness and love shines through her, even after the death of her husband and the murder of her sister, is still able to share the joy she has deep inside.

And Kimba, who, by her own admission, has done some terrible things, also seems filled with peace and joy.

I'm not sure I'll ever get to the point of finding any bit of happiness in this time of our lives.

I close my eyes as a wave of comfort passes through me. I may not be like these three women, but I realize I want to be. I want what they have.

As Kimba finishes her reading, she closes the Bible. "Jennifer, will you pray for our journey today?"

"Can I ask something first?" I raise my hand.

"Yes, of course."

"I understand the Bible reading. I mean, it makes sense that you read it so you can learn more about God, right?"

"Right, so we can learn about His character and also so we can grow."

"Okay. But why do you pray? I know it seems to make you all feel better to ask for, um, blessing on the food and on our travels or like when Donnie was shot. But does it really do any good? Do you ever *know* you get an answer?"

"Sometimes we do," Jennifer says. "In Donnie's case, we prayed, and he's alive and is expected to make a full recovery."

Leanne lets out a snort.

"But the main reason to pray," Jennifer continues, "is so we can spend time with God. I know you only see the outside prayers, the mealtime blessings and the ones we do before we start on the road. But for me, my private prayer time is the most amazing. That's not just when I'm petitioning God to help—though, I do often do that—but also when I'm thanking Him for what He has already done. And sometimes I'm just silent, basking in His glory. The power of prayer can be truly amazing."

I answer with a nod while my mind races. Could I pray for God to help me get over my guilt of marrying Jackson? Could I pray for him to help me with my grief over Dallas's death? Would He answer?

Jennifer asks if I have any more questions.

Even though I most definitely do, I tell her I don't.

She starts her prayer and even asks God to help me get any answers I may still have.

Once Jennifer finishes to a chorus of amens, Kimba pulls out her little calendar. She announces it's March 30th, then says, "If all goes well, we have two more nights on the road, then we'll be in Joliet."

"Since you insist on going there," Leanne says, "it's about time." Although her voice drips with contempt, something resembling a smile crosses her face and softens her words.

"No doubt." Rochelle snorts out a laugh.

Traveling on the paved road between Bridger and Fromberg is easy. We don't really need our skis with the skins attached, but we choose to wear them to help with traction on the icy spots. Donnie, who's still dealing with a massive headache, starts on his horse but quickly realizes the wagon is a better choice. Robyn also found a spot in the wagon.

Both of the young girls and Sebastian are shaken up over yesterday's shooting. Because of the clear road, Rey suggests the girls ski instead of riding in the wagon. He whispers the exercise might help them to not focus on the shooting.

When we stop at our first break, Sebastian asks if he can walk too. "I'll be super-duper careful so I don't fall." Because of him being so malnourished, the medical staff on the mountain didn't want him, his mom, or his sister walking until they no longer had the option of the wagon. When we reach Joliet, the skis my girls and I have will be passed on to them, but that leaves him with nothing for traction now.

"How big are your feet?" PJ asks.

"This big." Sebastian lifts a boot-clad foot in the air.

"Rochelle, do you think he could wear your cleats?"

"We might be able to cinch them up enough so they fit," she says.

After a few minutes of fiddling, Rochelle has the chain and spike contraction tightened as far as it'll go, which ends up being a little too tight to fit over Sebastian's snow boots. When he's finally set and we start traveling again, his smile covers his entire face.

We reach the outskirts of Fromberg shortly before lunch. After making sure we can take the road we need, the person at the roadblock informs us there's a campground on that edge of town if we're ready to stop for the day.

"I'm ready." Donnie lifts his bandaged hand. He really is quite a sight with the wrapped hand and head. Robyn, with her arm in a sling and looking pale, is also evidence we should call it a day. Only the three young children seem to still be full of energy, even after walking the seven miles between Bridger and Fromberg.

After setting up our camp, we talk about tomorrow.

"What is it, ten miles to Joliet?" Rey asks.

"I still think she'd be okay finishing this on her own," Leanne says. "I mean, I know you're all concerned she'll run in to trouble, but look how quiet it is here."

I stare at her and shake my head. "Have you forgotten what just happened in Bridger?"

She lifts a hand. "You eliminated that threat, proved that you're more than capable of not only taking care of yourself but the children too."

"I had help. Remember there was a guy with me?"

"Leanne," Rey says, shaking his head, "while I appreciate you discussing this rationally, you're beating a dead horse. We're not leaving Tamra and her children on their own. We'll deliver them properly, just like we'll deliver you properly to your aunt's house."

"I don't expect that. I'm not a fraidy cat unable to make the last several miles if it's out of your way."

"Thank you, Leanne," Kimba says. "I appreciate you thinking of the group like that. And I believe Tamra is just as considerate of everyone." She gives me a smile.

I want to respond with, *want to bet?* I'm totally okay with them going out of their way to see me home. But as Rey said, this has been discussed over and over. Leanne seems to be the only one with a burr in her side about it. Honestly, I thought maybe, after she stopped being so nasty to me, she'd let it go. Guess I was wrong.

Donnie, who I thought was napping in his tent, calls out, "Drop it, Leanne. Another couple of days doesn't make much of a difference now."

Letting out a loud sigh and shaking her head, Leanne pushes herself up from the ground and stomps away.

Chapter 22

Tonight, we're camped only a few miles outside of my childhood town of Joliet. I wanted to keep going, but that'd put us in Joliet as the sun's setting—not smart in today's world.

Travel was much slower today than on the highway between Bridger and Fromberg. This road is unplowed, so we're back to using our skis and skins, breaking trail as we trek.

The younger children went back to riding in the wagon, and Donnie was on his horse all day. He says his head still hurts, but it's not as bad as it was. I can't even imagine the headache that'd go along with such an injury.

Robyn, with her arm still aching, was squeezed into the wagon with Leanne and the children. Surprisingly, at one point in the day, Leanne told Robyn she should stretch out more and try to relax. To give her room, Leanne moved to a spot on a haybale.

The closer we get to home, the more butterflies fill my stomach. What will we find? Are my parents alive?

People in both Bridger and Fromberg said, as far as they know, Joliet is functioning similarly to their towns. There's even been some discussion of plowing the Joliet Fromberg Road to connect Joliet with the cooperative of Fromberg and Bridger. But with it now being the end of March, there's hope spring is on the horizon and the plowing isn't really needed. The massive storm that just went through suggests otherwise.

As we've all discussed ad nauseum, no one has ever seen a winter like this. With snow on the ground from October to March, it's certainly one for the record books.

What will the future look like? Will the president come through with his promises of turning the lights back on and ending lawlessness? Will people write memoirs of their experiences during this dark time, memoirs which will someday be considered history books? Or will we all choose to forget it?

Part of me wishes I would've kept a journal of the things that have happened, my thoughts and feelings of the events. Not all the events. I'd rather forget the day Dallas died, and the day I discovered Jackson was a murderer—a serial killer. And I'm not sure I'd ever want to read about shooting the lady wearing the tutu or her mother. Yeah, maybe it's better I'm not journaling. Some things are best forgotten.

Sitting alone around the camp stove as I tend to the supper, I let out a breath. There's so much I don't want to remember about this time, but some things I'll never forget. Like the way Jennifer has been toward me and my children, toward everyone really, even toward Icky—Victoria.

Somehow the nickname I gave her no longer feels right. Same with Leanne. While both may still fit their names, it leaves a sour feeling in the pit of my stomach when I try and use them. Oh, Leanne is still cantankerous most of the time. And Victoria's hygiene and behavior leaves a lot to be desired. But I realize the names, even if I don't announce them out loud, do more harm than anything. Maybe not to them, but to me.

While I may not be like Jennifer, Kimba, and Rochelle, committing myself to God, there's certainly something pulling me in that direction. The more I hear from them or from the Bible verses they read, the more I want to know. I feel a pull that I can't explain. Is it God? Jesus? My own curiosity?

Maybe, when I get to Joliet, I can find a Bible and read more on my own. Of course, my parents won't have one, but surely someone in town will have a spare.

I bite my lip as tears fill my eyes. I hope they're okay. Even with the belief the town itself is doing well, my parents are in their sixties. Neither had any severe health issues before, but things have changed so much in the last several months. Medical care and medicines are commodities. We're now living in a world where a simple infection can lead to death.

"They sound like they're getting closer." Robyn gingerly squats while attempting to keep her balance, her injured arm slung by her side, throwing her off slightly. The howl of at least two wolves echo through the small bowl we're camping in.

Like the night outside of Bridger, their song carries across the land. We could even hear them while we were in the little house in Bridger. But there's something different about hearing the wolves when in a tent compared to being in a house with doors and windows. It's eerie, and almost spooky, but also mystical.

It's not yet dark, with the sun tucked behind the mountain in the distance but still giving off plenty of light. After it drops completely, the wolf song will be even more ominous.

"Yeah, and they're the reason we're eating meager tonight." Donnie moves to the fire ring. "Those wolves are killing everything off."

Jameson Dawson saw a rabbit today and quickly brought it down with his .22 rifle. It was a jackrabbit and certainly nothing any of us would've ever wanted to eat before the world went dark, but as it stews, the aroma makes my mouth water. I offered a can of creamed corn to add to the stew, part of the rations I was given when we left the mountain.

The extra days in Bridger did nothing to help our food supply. We left the mountain with ration packages put together by the community, plus around a hundred pounds of dried venison. While on the road, we've supplemented with geese and small animals. Even so, many have expressed their concern. Along the river, in a sparsely populated area, the waterfowl is plentiful. When they reach the more populated towns, that'll stop.

Leanne has uttered several variations of I told you so. A look at her still malnourished frame makes me wonder how she'll even have the strength to keep going once Rochelle finds her son and she and PJ turn back with the team and wagon.

Leanne, and her equally skinny daughter, will then finish the rest of their hundred-mile-plus journey on foot. Can they even do it? At least Sebastian has seemed to flourish and regain some weight with our diet of fatty goose. With his brilliant smile and spunkiness, I can't help but like the boy.

Without the wagon, everyone will carry the bulk of their supplies on their backs as they tow the sleds. While a few in our group have decent backpacks, the kind used for multiday hikes and camping in the woods, the bulk are using a much more primitive version—from school-style bags to messenger bags that have been rigged to carry more than they should.

It won't be enough. At least they have the sleds so they can have a little bit of a stockpile. I half wonder if Leanne will crumple to the ground and Rey will end up throwing her on top of his sled just so they can make their miles each day.

No . . . she'd never allow it. The woman would keep moving, even if it meant her death, rather than give in to defeat. As much as I find her to be difficult and irksome, she's not a quitter. That much is clear.

As most of our group moves around the stove area, Robyn asks, "How far do you think the wolves range? Will we have problems with them closer to Billings?"

"Don't know." PJ shakes his head. "There's been the occasional wolf seen around there in the past few years as they extend their area."

"Yep, I wouldn't be a bit surprised," Donnie says. "Ever since they did the reintroduction, those wolves have gone where they've pleased."

"Wolves aren't that big of a deal," Jennifer adds. "We have a few packs around Great Falls. The grizzly bears, now that's a different subject."

"They're a big deal now," Donnie says, "just like we talked about the other night and just like the people in Bridger are discovering. You have a ranch, right? Did you lose any cattle to wolves?"

Jennifer shakes her head, while one of her sons say, "Not us, but a neighboring ranch had a wolf kill last winter. Lost a calf."

"See?" Donnie raises his uninjured hand.

"Well . . ." Atticus, the oldest of the A Boys, strokes the sparse beard on his chin. "He *said* he lost a calf. The fish and wildlife guy thought there might be some, um, discrepancies in his story."

"Oh, yeah," his brother says. "I forgot he was lying about it."

"You don't know that for sure," Jennifer corrects. "Our neighbor tends to exaggerate. He's . . . it's been challenging since he purchased the land a couple of years ago."

"Yeah, the guy tried to take part of our land," one of the A Boys say. "Had surveyors in and everything, thought his piece was bigger than it really is. He's not a nice guy."

"With the way things are, you can't afford to lose anything," Donnie says.

"I suspect wolves will be the least of our worries." Atticus looks to his mom. "We've been gone for so long, who knows what we'll find when we return. Our cattle might have already been taken."

"You had someone watching over the place?" Robyn asks, as she adjusts her position.

We're camped off the main road in a small group of trees. A downed log has been arranged for seating, and we've put a couple pieces of plastic on the ground as a barrier so those not on a log are off the snow.

"Our hired man," Jennifer says. "We pray he's all right. And we're also praying our neighbor has stepped up after realizing things are bad. Hopefully, he knows it's better to join forces than cause division."

The conversation continues, switching from the talk of the wolves to how things are now. Of course, how things are is kept lighter than how they really are since the children are doing what children do and hanging on to our every word—not that they haven't seen enough to know the truth. There's no denying the dangers we've encountered.

"I'm ready to stop sleeping in a tent," Debbie announces. "It stopped being fun."

"Last night for you." Sebastian smiles. "We'll be in tents for a lot longer. And pretty soon we won't even have the wagon to sleep in."

"Do you think we'll ever see you again, after you go to your aunt's and I stay with my grandma and grandpa?" Debbie asks.

"Sure we will." Sebastian nods vigorously. "Good friends stay good friends forever."

"Look," Robyn says in a soft voice.

I follow her finger across the field to a small bump on the landscape. "Oh!" The bump moves, revealing itself to be a wolf.

"Let me grab my rifle." Donnie quickly gets to his feet. "Too far for the pistol."

"What? No!" I cry. "She's not hurting anything. She's just watching us."

"The Bridger guy said wolves are shoot on sight."

"Let it go, Donnie," Rey says. "Tamra's right, she's just watching us."

"*Shoot on sight.* Do you know what that means?"

"Doesn't seem very sporting, though, does it? PJ, you're a hunter. What say you?"

I keep my eyes on the wolf. I've seen them in the wild before, but they're usually much darker than this one. She's almost white, barely noticeable against the snow. She's amazing and completely regal sitting on the mound.

"Look, Mommy!" Debbie says. "She's so beautiful."

"Great," Donnie scoffs. "Get the kids liking predators."

"Don't shoot, Donnie." PJ shakes his head. "While I agree with you that they're competing with us for food, I also agree with Rey. It's not very sporting. Plus, Debbie's right. She's beautiful."

Donnie spews off several choice words until Rey tells him to knock it off. Instead of sitting back in his spot, Donnie stomps off near the wagon and horses.

"Can he be trusted?" Robyn whispers.

"Yeah," Rey answers. "He'll do the right thing. Besides, his rifle's over there." He motions to a spot between the tents where a plastic cocoon holds Donnie's pack and rifle, not anywhere near the wagon and horses.

"Good. I was talking to one of the ladies at the medical clinic about the wolves. She's been speaking out against the killings, says it's time they had their freedom again. We don't need another slaughter like what happened to them before."

"Doesn't change the food issue," PJ points out.

"Surely there's a way to coexist," I say. "The indigenous people had a relationship with the wolves, right?"

"Exactly." Robyn bobs her head eagerly. "That's what the lady said. She said, if they could get along with them, we should be able to also. And she said— "

Whatever Robyn was going to add is lost when the sound of a rifle echoes through the camp. I grab Debbie, tossing her to the ground and throwing myself on top of her. As I'm trying to gather my wits, a second shot goes off. Too close. The shooter is too close.

"Donnie!" PJ screams.

"Stand down!" Rey yells. "Stand down now!"

"Mommy?" Debbie asks. "Is it over?"

"Did he . . . " Robyn starts in a shaky voice. "Oh, no."

I lift my head to look in the direction of the wolf.

"All right!" Jameson Dawson laughs. "Good shooting."

"You bunch of pansies weren't going to do it." Donnie smirks.

"He did the right thing," Leanne says. "There isn't enough food to go around. You've all had it so easy. You're soft. It's bad enough we have to compete with people who'll shoot back. There's no reason to give up our food to animals."

I move off Debbie and into a sitting position. Taking a deep breath, I mutter, "I'm not sure the wolf is the animal in this scenario."

"Nope," Donnie sneers. "The wolf is dead. And, hey, that's a mighty nice rifle you've got. I always wanted to try the Creedmore 6.5 caliber. I guess that worked out fine."

I'm on my feet in an instant and striding toward him. He's moved away from the wagon and closer to where we are, holding my rifle. The scoundrel took it out of the wagon and the case I keep it in overnight.

When I reach him, I hold out my hand for him to give it to me. As soon as I have a firm grip on it, I yank it away.

"Whoa. Touchy."

"You don't use anything that belongs to me without permission." I keep my voice low, willing myself to stay calm.

"No problem." He gives me an arrogant grin. "We'll be leaving you with your mommy and daddy tomorrow. I'm sure they'll be happy to tell you what a good little girl you've been. You can tell them how the big bad man stole your gun to kill the puppy dog."

"What's your problem? You've always been a little full of yourself, but you've never been an all-out jerk."

"This is the new Donnie." He puts his hands out to his side. "Almost dying made me realize life's too short for compromise."

"That right, mate?" Rey asks from a few feet away.

"That's right, limey. You might've been something back on the mountain, but I'm done taking orders from you. And I'm certainly not taking orders from a woman." He points to Kimba.

"Enough," Rey orders. "You have two choices, Donnie. Stop talking now and we'll move past this incident, or saddle up and ride away. Your call."

"He's done talking." Leanne rests a hand on his arm. "Aren't you, Donnie?"

He yanks his arm away from her.

Leanne steps closer, putting her hand back in place as she bores into him with her eyes. "It's just the headache, right?"

He closes his eyes. "Yeah. It's pretty bad."

"I bet it's making it hard to think straight."

"Right." Breaking eye contact with Leanne, he turns to Rey. "Tomorrow's a new day."

Leanne keeps her eyes on Donnie for another moment before turning on me. "This is your fault. The wolf is only dead because of you." Any pretense that we had a truce is quickly out the window.

"My fault? I didn't tell him to take my rifle and shoot it."

"It's your fault we're here. If we would've done the smart thing and left you on your own, this wouldn't have happened. Never forget, you killed the wolf."

"Leanne," Rey says in a sharp voice.

"People like her make me sick." She spins to face him. "They whine and carry on about an animal when people are dying around us."

She turns back to me. "You think I didn't see you moping around about killing that tutu-wearing lady? Who cares? Then getting sick over killing the old woman? You did the right thing. You protected those who couldn't protect themselves—my son, your daughter, his daughter." She points a boney finger in Rey's direction. "You felt bad about it, but you understood it was necessary. Are you going to make an animal's death something more than it is?"

With that, she spins and scurries back by the fire, plopping down in a huff.

Chapter 23

Taking down my tent in the early morning light, my gaze travels to the pile of rocks—the makeshift grave for the wolf. After last night, Donnie has been on his best behavior.

While Leanne did go to his defense and made sure to blame me for the entire fiasco, I think even she is still slightly disgusted with him. After her outburst, he made his way to sit next to her. She made a point of turning her body away from him. Is their little romance over?

The wolf killing bothered me. Maybe Leanne's right and I'm making more of it than I should. Just a few days ago, we watched as a man was shot in the head. A few minutes later I killed a woman, then her mom a few days after that. While these things have affected me deeply, the killing of the wolf feels remarkably similar. And I don't understand why. It's a wild animal, no different than a deer, an elk, or a goose—the exact things we've been killing to survive.

When Dallas used to go hunting, he'd bring home his harvest and we'd have a mini celebration. We didn't need the meat then to keep us fed; we could easily go to the grocery store and buy our food. Of course, it'd be naïve of me to think the meat from the grocery store didn't get there via the death of an animal too.

But this *feels* different.

"It's good we're getting an early start," Jennifer says, interrupting my wallowing. "Everyone's excited to reach Joliet today."

"It shouldn't take us long," I say. "I don't think we're more than two miles from Rock Creek at the edge of town."

"I'm sure you're thinking a lot about what we'll find there."

I blink rapidly as my eyes fill with tears. "I can't help but worry."

"Completely understandable. And while I'd like to tell you everything will be fine and your parents will be waiting to greet you, I can't give you that assurance."

I look at my boots as I continue to blink.

She touches my arm. "I thought you might be feeling concerned this morning. And I know you've been asking a lot of questions about God lately. I was wondering, do you have a Bible?"

"A Bible? No. At the services on the mountain when I'd sometimes attend, I'd use one of the Bible's they had on the table. I think I might try and find one in Joliet."

She gives me a smile. "Older women in the church are told to take the younger women under their wings. I should've done this when we first left the mountain—even while we lived up there. I knew you were struggling. I'm so sorry I never reached out to you before."

"Oh, you were . . . you were always kind to me. And you're not old, only a few years older than me."

"I don't know about not being old!" She laughs. "In today's world, with the loss of our medical advances, forty-nine is older than it was a year ago. Like Scruff said, we're practically in the Middle Ages, and life expectancy then was younger than I am now."

"Well . . . " I shrug.

"I want you to know, Tamra, if things aren't how you hope in Joliet, you're welcome to continue with us. We'd be happy to have you and your girls as part of our family. Of course, I don't know what we'll find either, but I do know we're determined to make our lives as full as possible."

My heart fills with gratitude from her offer. While I sincerely hope I don't need the option, it's wonderful to know we have this possibility. "Thank you, Jennifer."

"I'd also like to give you this." She reaches inside her zipped jacket and pulls out a book. "One of the ladies in Bakerville gave me this when my boys and I first arrived there. I'd like to pass it on to you."

She hands me the simple, gray book. "Won't you need it?"

"I have a small New Testament Bible that was my husband's. He carried it with him everywhere, so he had it on him when he was injured. When he died, I started carrying it with me. And each of my boys have a Bible, so we're set for our journey home."

"Thank you. I appreciate you giving this to me." I draw it close to my chest.

"I marked a passage I thought you might appreciate—to help with your questions about prayer. It's from Paul's writings to the church at Ephesus. Ephesians 6:18."

"Should I read it now?"

"You can. While this is only one example of how prayer is an important part of the life of a Believer, the entire book of Ephesians is well-worth reading. It shows how Jesus' work on the cross should permeate every aspect of our everyday lives, how we should serve in love of one another despite our differences." She gives me a small smile. "Paul called on the Church of Ephesus to love like Jesus."

With the Bible open to where she's left a scrap of paper and underlined the verse, I skim over it. "I may have heard this one of the times I went to the services on the mountain."

"It's certainly possible. Read it aloud and think on it today. But do go back and read the entire book. Like most verses, especially the more popular ones, it takes on a fuller meaning when read in context."

I clear the lump in my throat. "Praying at all times in the Spirit, with all prayer and supplication. To that end, keep alert with all perseverance, making supplication for all the saints."

"This version of the Bible is worded a little differently than some, but the meaning is still there," Jennifer promises. "I know you feel His calling. It's obvious in the questions you ask. You may feel unworthy, but keep in mind, we're all sinners. It's only through the blood of Jesus covering those sins we have salvation and eternal life with God."

Jennifer opens her arms and pulls me into a tight embrace. "I'm praying for you, Tamra, praying not only that your parents will be waiting with open arms but also that you come to know Jesus as your Lord and Savior."

~~~~~

My heart is pounding in my ears. Just a couple more bends in the road and we'll see the bridge entering Joliet. I'm certain I can already hear the creek bubbling around its ice covering.

When we left camp this morning, Debbie demanded she be allowed to skin into town. She wanted to be near the front of the line so she could be among the first to see Joliet.

While I understand her excitement, she won't see the town until after we know it's safe. She pouted over my decision for many minutes before Sebastian distracted her with a joke.

Unlike the completely wide-open area we encountered at the Bridger roadblock, this winding country road meanders around small hills, giving several opportunities for an ambush, according to Rey and Kimba.

"Tamra, are we getting close?" Rey asks, stopping his forward skinning.
~~~~~

"Yeah, not much farther. What do we want to do?"

"We'll do what we talked about earlier. Stop the wagon. Keep everyone here. We'll make first contact. You're still comfortable with that?"

I nod. "If they have a roadblock set up like the Fromberg folks said, I might know someone there."

"Agreed."

"Okay then, that's the plan," Kimba says. "Just like we talked about this morning, we'll stay behind this hillside."

"Should I turn the wagon?" PJ asks.

"Yep. And hand over the reins to Rochelle," Rey says. "Leanne has her rifle and is riding shotgun. Robyn and Victoria will keep the younger children down in the wagon. Nicole, you're also in the wagon with your rifle." Rey instructs his seventeen-year-old daughter. "Keep an eye on your sister and brother, okay?"

"Yes, of course," Nicole agrees, while her brother rolls his eyes.

Ignoring his children, Rey says, "Donnie, you know what to do?"

"Yup. Stay with the wagon."

"Right. Your head— "

"Don't worry none about me."

"All right, then. Everyone else is on foot and protecting the wagon. PJ, get your snowshoes on."

"You don't think we'll have any trouble, do you?" Victoria asks with a quiver in her voice.

"I hope not, but we're going to be ready."

I want to go to my girls, to hug them and hold them tight, to tell them I'll see them soon. But doing so would give credence to my fear and will scare them too. Instead, I straighten my shoulders and give them a cheery smile and a wave. "Be right back."

"Okay, Mommy." Debbie doesn't sound entirely convinced.

Beth gives me a single nod and her own small wave. Like Debbie, she looks less than confident about what happens next.

"It's just a precaution." I attempt a smile. My eyes fill with tears, but I quickly blink them away. "No different than how we approached the other towns."

"I know." Debbie sighs. "I'm just ready to be done."

"I'm with the kid," Donnie says. "Get on with it so we can be done for the day." He puts two fingers to the side of his head, massaging near the bullet wound.

Rey, who has been making final plans with Kimba, says, "Let's go then. Can't have Donnie getting any grumpier than he already is."

Donnie makes a face at him, turning his horse and moving to the front where the team of two is. His behavior garners a few quiet chuckles.

"See you soon." I wave to my girls as Rey and I take off on our skins.

"You ready?" he asks.

"I don't think we'll have any trouble." I will myself to believe it.

"We shouldn't," he agrees. "From what we've heard in Fromberg and Bridger, they're doing fine here, and it won't be a problem. But . . ."

"But no one has spoken to anyone from Joliet or been to the town since last month, and we know things can change quickly."

"In a heartbeat."

We discussed leaving our rifles and going in with only our sidearms. We thought we'd appear less threatening that way. Plus, if things go bad for us, our people might need the rifles for their defense.

We discarded both thoughts. In today's world, wearing a rifle is the normal thing. And if things do go bad and we're at a distance from the shooters, we'll need the rifles for our own protection.

I glance down at the Scout on my three-point sling. If I need to get to it quickly, I'll toss the ski poles and drop to my knee. I think through the process in my head while silently begging God not to make me need the rifle. I've done enough killing—too much. Will He listen to me even though I haven't accepted Him yet?

"Here we go," Rey says quietly as we make the last bend and come in full view of the well-manned roadblock. Rey stops our forward motion and gives a wave to the people at the creek. These people are smart—crouched down behind their cars. No one's standing up acting as a greeter.

"Howdy!" Rey yells out in his American voice. "Should we keep progressing?"

"C'mon ahead," one of the men calls back. "Be smart about it. We've got people everywhere."

I look at the hillside on the right and the open field on the left, along with the trees lining the river. I count four people, all armed and looking ready, in addition to at least three behind the cars.

"I'm Tamra Nicholson," I call out as we continue gliding forward. "My parents are Dennis and Hannah Reed."

The man who yelled out to us leans over toward one of the others. He scurries away. I swallow hard, trying to keep the nervousness from overwhelming me.

"Go ahead and come over here." The man beckons with his finger. "Keep your hands on your ski poles and away from your weapons."

"No problem," Rey answers. "We're not a threat to you."

When we're within thirty yards of the roadblock, the man says, "Stop there. You're Tamra Reed, huh?"

"I am." I attempt a wobbly smile. "Do you know my parents?"

"I know you too." He cocks his head, cracking a smile that shows his missing front tooth.

"Is that right?" Rey asks.

"Are you her husband?"

"I'm widowed. He's helping me and my children get home."

"Where are they?"

"What'd you say your name is?" I ask.

"CJ Bouchard. We went to school together."

"CJ, of course. It's been a while. I thought you moved to . . . somewhere."

"Yeah. Joplin, Missouri. I was home visiting my folks when everything went down, so now I'm here to stay."

"My parents?"

"Oh, yeah. I sent someone to let them know, figured I'd have time to vet you before they showed up."

"They're okay?" Tears spring to my eyes. "My parents?"

"They're fine. A little thin, but who isn't? I know they've been praying for you."

"They're fine!" I grab on to Rey's jacket, jumping up and down on my skis. "They're fine." I stop my movement and turn back to my high school friend. "Praying? My parents?"

"You'd better believe it. Your mom is what the preacher calls a prayer warrior. She knew you'd get here, said she was praying you home."

"My mom?"

"By God's grace, you're home, Tamra."

"I'm home. My mom prayed me home. *Thank you, God. Thank you, Jesus.*"

Thank you for spending your time with our weary travelers on their Montana journey! If you have five minutes, you'd make this writer very happy if you could write a short Amazon review.

I appreciate you!

The adventure continues in *Ruthless Havoc: Montana Mayhem Book 2*.

If your son were missing, what would you endure to find him?

Nine months ago, Rochelle's world turned upside down. Her son was away at summer camp when the lights went out.

Then things went from bad to worse.

Her husband was murdered as she watched. She and her daughters were taken captive, then sold to the highest bidder.

Now that she and her girls are free, and spring is on the horizon, it's time to find her son.

But this new world is full of hazards, and being on the road heightens the danger. They say there's safety in numbers, so traveling with a group should provide protection. That's not always the case. Sometimes even people you know can be a threat.

Ruthless Havoc, Book 2 of the highly anticipated follow-up series to the bestselling *Havoc in Wyoming* Christian Futuristic series, follows the societal collapse in Big Sky Country. Featuring engaging scenarios, riveting action, and flawed yet strong and complex women, the *Montana Mayhem* series is perfect for fans of Mark Goodwin, Jamie Lee Grey, and Kyla Stone.

Some people in our traveling group left behind close friends or family when beginning their journey off the mountain. Read more about the adventures on the mountain, and before, in the *Havoc in Wyoming* series.

Havoc in Wyoming

Part 1: Caldwell's Homestead

Jake and Mollie Caldwell started their small farm and homestead to be able to provide for an uncertain future for their family, friends, and community. They have tried to plan for everything. They never planned on Mollie being away on business when the terrorists attacked.

Part 2: Katie's Journey

Katie loves living on her own while finishing up her college degree, working her part-time jobs, and building a relationship with her boyfriend, Leo. When disaster strikes, being away from family isn't quite so nice, and home is over a thousand miles away. Will she make it home before the United States falls apart?

Part 3: Mollie's Quest

Two or three times a year, Mollie Caldwell travels for business. Being away from her Wyoming farmstead is both a fun time and a challenge. They started their farm to be able to provide for an uncertain future for their family, friends, and community. The farm keeps the entire family busy, meaning extra work for her husband while she's away. This time, while on her business trip, terrorists attack. Her weeklong business trip becomes much longer as she tries to make her way home.

Part 3.5: Havoc Begins

Laurie Esplin is spending summer break from college in her hometown of Wesley. As far as she's concerned, this small town--full of kind people--is just about heaven on earth. Her fiancé Aaron makes it even better. When a series of terrorist attacks happen, Laurie is concerned but is positive they're safe in Wesley. She's wrong.

Part 4: Shields and Ramparts

The United States, and the community of Bakerville, face a new threat . . . a threat that could change America forever. As the neighbors band together, all worry about friends and family members. Have they found safety from this latest danger?

Part 5: Fowler's Snare

Welcome to Bakerville, the sleepy Wyoming community Mollie and Jake Caldwell have chosen as their family retreat. At the edge of the wilderness, far away from the big city, they were so sure nothing bad could ever happen in such a protected place. They were wrong. Now, with the entire nation in peril, coming together as a community is the only way they can survive. But not everyone in the community has the people of Bakerville's best interest at heart.

Part 5.5: Havoc Rises

Newlyweds Shelby and Grant Cameron are expecting their first child. But their excitement over the upcoming birth is shadowed by a series of terrorist attacks. Shelby's concerns are increased when the town's hospital burns down. Their small Wyoming town begins to pull together as plans are made for the future. Things are going well until one fateful night when everything changes.

Part 6: Pestilence in the Darkness

Surrounded by danger, they band together with the community of Bakerville to move to a new defensible location. But they weren't prepared to have to give up so much for the security they so desperately need. And they quickly learn trust must be earned, not freely given.

Part 6.5: Havoc Peaks

When their small community in Oregon is overrun with refugees from the nearby cities, Clarice and her family assume they will band together with their neighbors. As the other families mysteriously disappear, it soon becomes evident the only option is to leave. But the only safe place they know is over 1000 miles away. Will the journey prove too dangerous?

Part 7: My Refuge and Fortress

When Jake and a group of hunters return to Bakerville and find their former neighbors slaughtered, they realize there is a new, even more deadly threat. Will their reinforced location be secure enough? And what about the radio announcement from the president? Will his promise of help arrive in time?

Find these titles on Amazon:
www.amazon.com/author/milliecopper

Acknowledgments

Thanks to:

Ameryn Tucker, my editor, beta reader, and daughter wrapped in one. I had a story I wanted to tell, and Ameryn encouraged me and helped me bring it to life.

Dee from Dauntless Cover Design.

My husband, who gave me the time and space I needed to complete this dream and was very patient as I'd tell him the same plot ideas over and over and over.

Three more daughters and a young son, who willingly listen to me drone on and on about story lines and ideas while encouraging me to "keep going."

My amazing Beta Readers! Thanks to April, Becky, Delia, Karl, Katrina, Kristina, Linda, Glen, Wes, Barbara, Tonya, and Tammy for your help in creating the final story. Your insights and abilities to see the things I miss are very much appreciated! And a special thank you to Tim, specialist in all things that go boom, for always answering my questions and pointing out things I wouldn't even think about.

And to you, my readers, for spending your time with our band of weary travelers. If you have five minutes, you'd make this writer very happy if you could leave a review. I appreciate you!

About the Author

Millie Copper, writer of Cozy Apocalyptic Fiction and preparedness mentor, was born in Nebraska but never lived there. Her parents fully embraced wanderlust and moved regularly, giving her an advantage of being from nowhere and everywhere.

Millie Copper lives in the wilds of Wyoming with her husband and young son, tending chickens and attempting a food forest on their small homestead. After living off the grid for several years, they've recently gone back on the grid. Four adult daughters, three sons-in-law, four grandchildren, and one more on the way round out the family.

Since 2009, Millie has authored articles on traditional foods, alternative health, homesteading, and preparedness-many times all within the same piece. Millie has penned seven nonfiction, traditional food focused books, sharing how, with a little creativity, anyone can transition to a real foods diet without overwhelming their food budget.

The twelve-installment *Havoc in Wyoming* Christian Post-Apocalyptic fiction series uses her homesteading, off-the-grid, and preparedness lifestyle as a guide. The adventure continues with the newly released *Montana Mayhem* series.

Find Millie at www.MillieCopper.com
Facebook: www.facebook.com/MillieCopperAuthor/
Amazon: www.amazon.com/author/milliecopper
BookBub: https://www.bookbub.com/authors/millie-copper